J. G. Donnelly

Jesus Delaney

A novel

J. G. Donnelly

Jesus Delaney
A novel

ISBN/EAN: 9783744646871

Printed in Europe, USA, Canada, Australia, Japan

Cover: Foto ©Andreas Hilbeck / pixelio.de

More available books at **www.hansebooks.com**

JESUS DELANEY

A NOVEL

BY

JOSEPH GORDON DONNELLY

New York
THE MACMILLAN COMPANY
LONDON: MACMILLAN & CO., Ltd.
1899

WRITTEN EN ROUTE

OFF at last! It is now full ten years since a lecture by the Reverend Luther Lamb, a missionary, gave me the idea of visiting Mexico. Such a queer people he described — and his great work among them rooting out the old faith and planting the new!

I was not what you would call a church man (few of us are on 'Change), still I deemed it my duty after that lecture to join the Mission League, — this, too, against the protest of my partner, Brown, whose home mission hobby even then was a by-word with the boys.

Brown has statistics that are very tedious, of 1,500,000 drunkards, 300,000 chronic criminals, and Heaven knows how many bad men and women of all sorts, whose reform, he says, needs the best efforts of all of us in our own land and at our own doors. And he has a fable which he tells so often every one on 'Change knows it by heart. It runs thus : —

" BROWN'S FABLE

" Once there was a Good Dog who took it in his head that wolves were dogs run wild, and that if they had the right sort of care when young they would be dogs. So this Good Dog left his own pups (some of which were none too good), and went to a Strange Land where he found a wolf cub. He took the cub home with him, and taught it to live like a dog. In course of time it could stand on its hind legs, raise its paws, and bark and roll its eyes as if in speech or prayer. When full grown, he brought it back to the Strange Land, that it might teach the wolves there to live like dogs. But night came, and it heard the far-off cry of wolves and tried to go to them. And when the Good Dog strove to hold it back, it snarled and bit him, and went off. It was still a wolf."

A hard-headed man, Brown, and kind at heart ; but like all people of the sort, he lacks breadth.

I have never had reason to lose faith in the mission cause, or lessen my interest in the work of the Reverend Lamb and his colaborers in Mexico.

But one thing or another has put off my trip there until now. Free from business and family cares (alas! that such freedom so seldom comes with the capacity to enjoy it!), and advised by physicians that the change will do me good, I have boarded a train for the land of the Montezumas.

Brown was at the depot to see me off.

" Don't bother writing letters," said he. " Keep tab in your own way."

I shall do so.

CONTENTS

CHAPTER		PAGE

CONTENTS   xi

JESUS DELANEY

CHAPTER I

JESUS DELANEY

"You must send it to me by Jesus."

Such was the closing sentence of a note from the Reverend Luther Lamb just delivered to me at the Hotel San José in Alameda.

I was shocked and puzzled. Of course this was Mexico, where odd things may be looked for. Elsewhere in the world civilization and barbarism are at war — here they seem to be on the best of terms, cheek by jowl. Although less than two days in the country, I have seen with my own eyes blanketed Indians in the streets saluting each other with the elegant courtesy of Spanish grandees, cultured ladies in a street car smoking cigarettes and puffing the smoke from mouth and nose, uniformed soldiers on dress parade barefooted, a beggar on horseback asking alms, a farmer ploughing by electric light and using for a plough a forked stick as in the days of Abraham, naked cave-dwellers within earshot of a printing press. I have heard of bull rings in the shadow of cathedrals, priests presiding at cock-fights — "at every hand," as written in the *Mission Clarion*, "much of modern progress, but more of the demoralization of Romanism and revolution."

Sights of this sort are apt to mix one's sense of what's becoming, and Brother Lamb had lived here in charge of the Mission Institute for over a dozen years. Yet even so, that a Christian minister, a missionary in fact whose sacred work it was to lift the Mexican masses, should use such language was inconceivable. What could possess him? There was no excuse for it. I had merely forgotten to send him a book which I had promised the evening before. Surely a little lapse like that was the last thing in the world to provoke profanity.

Thus pondering on the note, I chanced to look up at the young Mexican who had delivered it.

"Is Brother Lamb," I began, then recollecting that I must speak in Spanish, I paused to put together the sentence, "Is Brother Lamb well?"

You would think that this ought to be an easy matter for one who, when a boy, had a two years' course in Spanish at the Naval Academy. Indeed I passed for a linguist around home, and some weeks before starting for Mexico had taken up "Spanish at a Gulp" to put the finishing touches on my fluency. But the language faculty failed me the moment I crossed the border; at the first rattle of the real article from the lips of a Mexican Customs officer, I was stricken deaf, dumb, and tongue-tied.

Even the equivalents of these four simple words had to be laboriously sought and dubiously dragged forth:—

"Esta Brother Lamb — I mean — Hermano Lamb bien?"

"Si, señor, muy bien."

The reply was curiously soft and musical, and I could not help noticing the gracious courtesy which seemed unconscious of my broken speech.

Then I essayed, "Are you connected with the Mission Institute?" getting it like this, "Esta Vd. connected — I mean — conectado — ah! — con la Instituto de misionario?"

I knew it was abominable Spanish, but he understood and answered at once:—

"Si, señor, fui uno de los primeros discipulos del Instituto; recibi mi diploma y soy ahora asistente profesor del Reverendo Lamb."

For the life of me I could not catch his meaning. It was aggravating. "Confound it," said I in an undertone, "why can't such an intelligent-looking young fellow talk like a Christian?"

"Would you rather I spoke English, sir?" came the smiling query of the Mexican, without the slightest trace of a foreign accent.

"Oh! You are an American," I exclaimed.

"No, sir; I am a Mexican."

I recalled the warning a Pullman conductor had given me on the way down, "Beware of a Mexican who talks English, or a negro who talks Spanish;" so I took a sharp look at this English-speaking Mexican.

He had a good face, just enough bronzing of the olive to suggest the native cross with the Spaniard, nose slightly aquiline, an amiable mouth, a strong, shapely chin, and large brown-black eyes. He had the straight hair of the Indian and his pose and figure somehow brought to my mind Cooper's description of the Delaware Chief — this in spite of the fact that he was dressed in plain black clothes of a clerical cut.

"Are you connected with the Mission Institute?" I asked.

"Yes," he replied; "I was one of the first graduates and am now acting as Brother Lamb's assistant. He told me you had promised him a very interesting book and he wished you to send it to him by me."

"Ah! Yes! Send it by you!"

I reread the note and light began to break.

"By the way, may I inquire your name?"

"Jesus Delaney."[1]

"Jesus!"

I must have surprised the young man by laughing aloud and shaking him cordially by the hand.

"My name sounds strangely to American ears," he remarked good-naturedly.

"It doesn't sound as bad as it looks," I responded and, showing him the note, he at once understood and joined in my merriment.

This was not the first time I had heard of Jesus Delaney. He had been mentioned to me by the Reverend Lamb as the ripest fruit of his harvest — he had been named from time to time in the Mission Reports as one from whom great results were expected, and a recent paragraph in the *Clarion* told how he had lately come back to Alameda after five years at a Northern college.

I was indeed pleased to meet him. Here was living proof of what mission work could accomplish.

---

[1] Jesus, pronounced Haysus, accent on last syllable, is a common name in Mexico.

" The Reverend Lamb has spoken to me of you,"
said I.

" The Reverend Lamb has also told me of you,"
he replied, " and how much you have done for our
Institute."

He spoke easily and with an unaffected modesty
and dignity of manner.

" I know," he went on, " it is to you and others
like you I owe what I am " (there was deepening
earnestness in look and tone), " and it will be my
life-work to prove that I am not ungrateful — that
your benevolence was not misplaced."

His voice faltered and the big eyes dimmed.

" I believe you, my boy, I believe you," said I,
hastily.   " So you like your work ? "

As if the fire of faith were suddenly stirred, his
handsome face lit up.

" Like it ?   I love it ! " he exclaimed.   " My
country is politically free, but spiritually enslaved.
Surely, if it were God-like to rebel against Spain,
it is now the patriot's part to raise the standard of
revolt against Rome."

Read in these pages the young man's speech
may seem theatrical — heard from his lips with the
accompaniment of flashing eyes and impassioned
gesture, it seemed inspired.   If Brown could only
have been there to see and hear !

"And have you hopes of victory?" I asked.

"It is more than hope, it is faith," he answered. "I know I shall live to see my race redeemed."

And he went on to speak of the changed condition of Mexico, the political stability, the liberal ascendancy, how her people were awakening from the torpor of centuries. "Progress," he concluded, "is in the air."

Even as he spoke, I saw passing an ox-team dragging an ancient two-wheel cart, the poor beasts yoked by the horns with thongs of rawhide.

"It may be in the air," thought I, "but certainly — " he divined my reflections.

"Yes, but look beyond at that locomotive flying by with its palace cars," he said, his splendid eyes aglow. "There goes an old-time water carrier, his jars hanging from his shoulders, but mark how he stops at that hydrant to fill them. Right in the path of the lowliest lives modern methods are making headway. Tell our northern friends that the Bible has reinforcements. Steam and electricity are missionaries."

"Protestant missionaries?" I asked.

"Thoroughly Protestant! Every incandescent flash, every whirr of wheels and screech of whistle, is a protest against Popery." Which sentiments were dear to my heart.

"There's a war-cry!" he remarked jocularly, as a long fierce blast from some factory tore through the soft chimes of the great cathedral.

It was interesting to note the happy intuition with which he anticipated. But what most surprised and delighted me was his odd way of blending unrelated ideas, his quick shifts from grave to gay, and a certain playful humor that bubbled and sparkled in his various moods. It was so unlike anything I had been led to look for in a Mexican that I became curious about his pedigree.

"Something in your manner and appearance, Mr. Delaney —"

"Please call me Jesus," he interrupted. "I can scarcely recognize myself by any other name."

"Something in your manner makes me ask: Are you a full-blooded Mexican?"

"It is as hard to say what constitutes a full-blooded Mexican as what constitutes a full-blooded American," he answered.

Recalling the commingling of English, French, Dutch, and German in myself, I had to bow assent.

"My mother," he continued, "traces her ancestry to the Aztec Cacique Ichichuatl, who wedded a Spanish maiden."

"And your father?"

" My father never went farther back than my grandfather, Don Patricio Delaney."

" Don Patricio ? A Mexican ? "

" An Irish-Mexican. But Don Patricio once told my mother that his ancestors were Irish kings."

Jesus spoke of his royal origin, Aztec and Hibernian, with such grave conviction, I did not smile.

He was full of the traditional glories of his country ere the coming of Cortes, and as he told the stirring legends, one could almost imagine him with flashing spear and shield of gold leading some predatory band of warriors. But he was charming. Indeed, when he rose to leave, I was reluctant to part with him. And that evening, when the Reverend Lamb called to talk over the affairs of the Institute, I seized the first chance to change the subject so that he might tell me more of Jesus Delaney.

CHAPTER II

EVOLUTION OF A MISSIONARY

THE Reverend Lamb has a good hearty hate of Rome. He says he inherited it from ancestors who fought and prayed with Cromwell. If so, it has lost nothing in the process of transmission. No matter what the topic, he is sure to find some opening for thrust or stroke at his ancient foe.

While telling me the simple story of Jesus Delaney, so frequent were his raids into the enemy's territory, I found it hard to follow him. But by sounding repeated recalls, I managed before midnight to get a fair account of this young Mexican in whom I have become greatly interested.

Jesus Delaney was the first Mexican boy secured by the Mission Institute; he was then eight years of age. The letter of the Reverend Lamb announcing the fact is a cherished record at the League Headquarters. "God be praised!" he wrote, "a boy brand has been snatched from the maw of the scarlet woman."

The father of Jesus had died leaving widow and son without means. In his lifetime they had never known want, — for while Don Miguel (as the father was called) had no regular profession and seldom steady employment, he always managed to be doing something somehow. Once he obtained a position on the police force, and when the news was communicated to Don Patricio (paternal-grand-father of Jesus) the aged man chuckled in his odd Spanish and English (both of which, Reverend Lamb says, he spoke with a brogue): —

"Bueno! Bueno! Stick to that, Moike! A cousin of mine as was polisman in Nueva York para dos años is ahora un gran caballero."

But Don Miguel did not heed his father. He chafed under the discipline prescribed by the Ayuntamiento, and finally lost his place through a fierce assault with his club on the pate of the Jefe Politico, Don Esteban José Maria Vicario. For a time before his death he held the office of Alcalde, drawing a good salary, but as was always the case, lived beyond his income, while his wife, Doña Concepcion Morel de Delaney, supplemented his extravagance with her own improvidence.

She was a well-bred woman, daughter of Colonel Villareal, a patriot soldier, and never knew the need of money before marriage, nor the use of it afterward. Still it was the proud boast of Don Miguel that he had the handsomest wife and boy in Alameda.

His death was deeply deplored by countless friends and creditors; vehicles had to be hired from adjoining towns to supply the demand for his funeral, which it is well known was only exceeded in length, pomp, and circumstance by that of the deceased Don Patricio.

The widow made some effort to keep up appearances by the sale or pledge at the monte pio of wearing apparel and furniture. But this resource was soon exhausted and she had to seek employment.

Jesus was in the way.

Don Pedro Sanchez, who needed a governess for his children, would have no encumbrance in the shape of a boy. Doña This and Doña That who wanted her services expressly stipulated she must stay at their respective houses, away from her son. Alone, many a door was open; with Jesus, there was no admittance.

It was at this time she met the wife of Reverend Lamb, who, seeing her strait, offered to take Jesus and make him an educated gentleman. She showed the mother the bright rooms, the well-provided table, the pretty uniform, and introduced the kindly faced ladies who were her assistants.

It was a godsend — Jesus went to the Institute, and soon became the pet of all, particularly of Mrs. Lamb. With him went Antonio, an old family servant who had been his nurse and companion from birth.

Every Saturday came the mother, and they spent an hour together — an hour of that love which of all love is holiest. There was trouble at first from her visits, as she frequently smuggled to the boy little leaden Madonnas, pictures of saints, medals, and scapulars that were justly an abomination in the sight of the Reverend Lamb. But he managed to seize and confiscate these until such time as Jesus had been taught better, when, although he would not wound his mother's feelings by refusing her gifts, he gratified his teachers by their prompt exposure and delivery.

At the age of fifteen he had completed the Institute curriculum, and was transferred to the Evangelical University in the United States, where he spent five years. He wrote weekly to his mother, and to Mrs. Lamb whom he loved as a mother, monthly to the Reverend Lamb, and also frequent letters to Antonio, who could neither read nor write, yet treasured the correspondence as a miser his gold.

The college career of Jesus was fairly satisfactory. He earned no great distinction as a student, but he was very popular with his fellows. It is admitted that he was more devoted to the gymnasium than to his books, and became easily first in all athletic exercises. An intimacy soon developed between him and the Professor of Physical Culture (who had been at one time a famous athlete), and it was discovered too late that the Professor had taught Jesus the ungodly art of self-defence — in fact trained him in the use of gloves and foils until he was more proficient than his master.

He was prone to fits of temper. There is a dark story to the effect that one day, alone with the Reverend Ichabod Deusnap, his tutor in Moral Philosophy, the latter reflected on the virtue of Mexican women. Jesus sprang up with a Spanish oath, drew a knife on the terrified tutor, and forced from him an abject apology. But the Reverend Deusnap denies the story and Jesus doesn't admit it.

On the other hand, he was honorably mentioned by the local humane society, for the brave rescue of a helpless chicken from a savage bulldog, although an anonymous letter to the Reverend

Lamb charged that the chicken was subsequently entered by Jesus at a cocking main.

Lassoing Doctor Twombley was his most serious escapade. The venerable Doctor, distinguished for old-school gallantry, had just bidden elaborate farewell to some ladies who were gathered on the front porch, and was hastening gayly along the walk when a coiled clothes-line came circling down upon him, fastened his arms helplessly and drew him, speechless with indignation, to a sitting posture.

The closest watch and strictest orders failed to cure him of a habit he had of leaping the fence of the college campus into Deacon Oldney's pasture and cutting up all sorts of risky capers with the Deacon's bull. He would wave a red handkerchief before its eyes and dodge its fierce charges. He was known even to seize its tail until the furious beast whirled to a standstill, when he would vault upon its back and romp madly round the pasture.

He had an unaccountable passion for tight pantaloons, large buttons, high hats, and profuse silver ornaments. Checked and suppressed, and at times supposed to be completely conquered, this passion would break out in violent form when least expected.

But all in all, it appeared from Reverend Lamb's account, Jesus did well at the University and left it with a cultured mind and a heart fervent for the faith. The Reverend Lamb pictured as an affecting scene the occasion of his graduation, when the aged President, before presenting his diploma, related to the assembled multitude the touching story of his life, and described his devoted country "writhing in the ravenous clutches of Rome."

"In God's name," said the President, in closing, "I now send forth to Mexico's rescue, glorious as a knight of old and clad in the armored panoply of the Gospel, her son and our brother, Jesus Delaney."

CHAPTER III

THE day following my meeting with Jesus I made my first visit to the Mission Institute. It is conveniently situated in a central part of the city. Buildings and grounds cover a whole square, and before the main structure is laid out a little park with great trees, tropical plants, winding walks, and beautiful flower beds. Entering this park from the street, I made my way to the main door, where an aged Mexican servant sat on the porch, absorbed in a large volume which lay upon his knees. He looked up as I approached, smiled amiably, and resumed his reading. The face he disclosed was cruelly disfigured by a harelip and a deep scar on the right cheek; yet its expression when he smiled was strangely benign and child-like. The book, I could see, was a Bible. It was a most gratifying sight; it filled my mind and quickened my heart. That dark face seemed to reflect the sacred light of truth; that poor benighted mind was illuminated.

"Who," thought I, "can measure the worth of this one soul redeemed? What cost in sordid gold —"

"You are welcome to the Institute," said a soft, pleasant voice, and Jesus came forward with extended hand. I pointed to the aged Mexican, still bent over his Bible.

"There," said I, "there is the most touching thing I have witnessed since coming to Mexico, that old man reading his Bible."

Jesus surprised me by a merry laugh.

"That! Why, that's Antonio. He isn't reading; he can't read. He's just looking at the pictures."

"Antonio!" He addressed the old man in Spanish, at the same time examining the volume over his shoulder.

"Que estas mirando?"

Antonio laughed a low, gleeful laugh without looking up and answered : —

"El soldado tiene al niño por los pies y lo va a cortar en dos. Esta gritando y pataleando y la madre tambien grita."

"It is the picture of Solomon deciding which is the mother of the child," explained Jesus. "Antonio enjoys the sight of the soldier holding the child up by the heels as if about to cut it in two. You see —"

"Is Brother Lamb in?" I interrupted. The truth when it spoils a nice illusion is trying to one's temper.

Brother Lamb was very cordial. In fact he made a little speech as he pressed both my hands.

"It gives me pleasure," said he, "to welcome to the Institute one whom I know to be interested in its work, and to have contributed so generously to its advancement."

He took me through the dormitories, dining rooms, kitchen, classrooms, and chapel, showed me the beautiful patio which the building enclosed, and lastly the quarters reserved for himself and family.

Brown might have looked askance at the comforts and even elegancies of the latter — the rugs and furnishings were luxurious, the curtained beds restful, and servants in waiting at every step; but such evidences of good living pleased me. Of course I could not help contrasting it all with the stinted little cottage which the Reverend Lamb occupied when pastor at Zionville, where I first knew him, and where he had a flock notoriously tenacious of its fleece. But so much the better for the Reverend Lamb. Missionaries, like other men, are capable of better work the better they are housed and cared for. The man of Galilee? Well, that was eighteen centuries ago, and Galilee isn't Mexico (though said to look like it).

Most interesting of all to me were the children, fully a hundred, some bright and intelligent, others not so promising; in age, from infancy to young womanhood; in color, from chocolate to cream. It did my heart good to look at them and think of the change being wrought in their young lives, and how in every land throughout the world, holy men like the Reverend Lamb were thus spreading the Gospel.

"This was formerly a nunnery," said Reverend Lamb. "Where now you see these happy maidens gathered in the glow of evangelical Truth, poor blinded women were once shut up, their souls congealed in superstitious darkness."

The good man's face beamed with honest pride — here was the fruition of his years of labor.

We were standing in the main hallway looking at the patio into which the children were just marching arm in arm, keeping step to the music of an organ, their faces wreathed in smiles and their black eyes sparkling. They circled round the playing fountain, and as the first couple passed us the fresh young voices were raised in a tuneful Mexican hymn. It was indeed a pretty sight. I watched till the last child disappeared from view and strove to hold the last sweet echo of their song.

"You must love this work," said I.

"It is God's work," he answered. "Every one of these .children is a brand snatched from the burning, a soul saved from the blighting claws of Rome, a future worker in the Lord's vineyard."

"And your wife? Does not the exile wear on her?"

"Wear upon her! Here she comes with our boy. Does she look worn?"

The lady approaching was the last person in the world I would have taken for the wife of the Reverend Lamb. I knew, of course, that Mrs. Lamb was regularly enrolled as a missionary, but no mention being made of her in the reports (indeed you only came across her name on the quarterly pay-rolls) I supposed her to be a quiet homebody devoted to domestic rather than missionary duties.

Here, however, was a distinguished-looking woman. Very tall, she had the graceful carriage that only goes with perfect physical proportions, and her snow-white hair heightened the almost youthful beauty of her face — a face noble and intellectual in its every line. There could be no mistaking her sympathetic nature — expression, voice, manner, breathed the same sweet harmony. No note of self —her very presence encompassed you with considerate kindliness.

The Reverend Lamb rallied her on my remark about exile.

"When I first came here, I was too busy to be homesick ; " said she, smiling, " there were — "

" Souls all about to be saved," interposed the Reverend Lamb.

" Bodies all about to be fed and cleaned and clad," she continued, and her large, velvety black eyes gave the glow of a soul consecrate to Charity.

She had a soft, soothing voice, such a voice as lulls a child or lures a man. I loved to listen to it.

"I have lived here so long now, Alameda is my home, her people my people, and their uplifting my life-work."

"But this little boy of yours ? In a few years more he must have other advantages and associations than you can afford him here. You would not sacrifice his future to the mission cause ?"

She stroked the lad's glossy hair a moment as if in deep thought, but before she could reply the Reverend Lamb again answered, "Yes ! Should the Lord so demand, even our beloved child," and his eyes were raised and his lips moved in silent prayer.

Into the narrow groove in which my life had run so many years there flashed that sentiment sublime! I praised God that men were still on earth like the Reverend Lamb.

CHAPTER IV

THE MISSION TEA

I HAD tea with the faculty, consisting of the Reverend and Mrs. Lamb, Jesus and four ladies. Three of the latter, whose names I did not catch, but whom I distinguished in the order of their introduction as Nos. 1, 2, and 3, were very young. Had they dressed for a ball instead of a plain mission tea, their costumes would not have been much more elaborate; what with ribbons, lace, frills, and frippery, it was hard to believe them missionaries. Reverend Lamb must have noticed my surprise, for he made a whispered explanation : —

"We have so few visitors. The young ladies regard this as quite an occasion."

So it was done on my account, if overdone, and besides (I bethought me), dress goods are cheap in Mexico, and — well, women are women the world over. I greeted the girls kindly.

" It was brave in ladies so young as you to leave home and friends, and come to this foreign land."

They seemed unduly affected.

"Do people really talk of us?" asked one.

"People everywhere admire the courage and zeal of our noble women missionaries," I responded gallantly.

"Oh my!" came in a self-conscious chorus, and the way they blushed and beamed showed they could take more. I could not help thinking how much better fitted they would be for mission work in Mexico, had they some slight share of that easy courtesy, that graciousness and self-possession of manner so common in the humblest classes of Alameda.

"Do you enjoy life here?" I inquired.

"Not so much as at first," said No. 1.

"The novelty wears off," said No. 2.

"But we have lots of fun yet," said No. 3.

These replies jarred on me and must have been displeasing to the Reverend Lamb, for he abruptly drew me aside to introduce the fourth lady, a Miss Anderson.

"A wonderful woman," he had previously remarked. "Devoted to the mission cause, and — rich."

The last quality, her wealth, was mentioned with a lowering of voice and brows that was impressive and peculiar.

Miss Anderson had ceased to be young. She

had a strong face, keen eyes, and the deep lines
and leathery color which tell of prolonged service
in the schoolroom.   But the remarkable thing
about her was her voice, deep and clear; coming
from a woman of only moderate size, it startled me
when she spoke.   She seemed the monitor of the
faculty, alert for every lapse.

During the meal, the Reverend Lamb commented on Mexican mythology.

"The ancient God of the Mexicans was Hetzal-
coatl," he remarked.

"Quetzalcoatl," corrected Miss Anderson.

"Ah! Yes! Quetzalcoatl — of course, Quetzalcoatl," said the Reverend Lamb.

"Now, they worship the Virgin Mary," said
No. 1.

"The Virgin of Guadalupe," from Miss Anderson.

"I mean the Virgin of Guadalupe," mildly
assented No. 1.

"Just a change of idols," simpered No. 2.

"I really prefer the old idol to the Madonna,"
giggled No. 3.

"Your idol would naturally be a man," said
Jesus, whereupon Nos. 1, 2, and 3 became
hysterical.

"If we must have idols," said I, good humoredly.

"Must have idols!" repeated with reproving voice, Miss Anderson.

"Ah! I mean as between idols, I prefer to worship the beauty, sweetness, and sanctity of woman."

"Worship!" Miss Anderson's powerful pronunciation was a protest which drove me into an immediate, although confused, apology. From that on I was on my guard.

"The ancient Aztecs had a female idol — Tonteotl," said Reverend Lamb.

"Centeotl," corrected Miss Anderson.

Reverend Lamb meekly concurred.

"In their legend of the creation," he continued, "they have it that God first made man out of straw — "

"Wood!" said Miss Anderson.

"Ah! — Yes! out of wood." The Reverend Lamb never disputed her amendments.

"Does this legend account for the number of wooden men?" I inquired. My sally was taken seriously by Nos. 1, 2, and 3, who looked puzzled, as if the question were put to them.

"Possibly the number of wooden men accounts for the legend," said Jesus.

I observed that Miss Anderson never corrected Jesus. On the contrary, she seemed to esteem his levity beyond its merits. But she spared no one else. Her memory was amazing, ranging over the whole field of conversation with the quick eye and sharp talons of a hawk. Once I ventured a personal experience which occurred during the Rebellion, and a little harmless misstatement was descried by her and pounced upon.

"Why, my dear lady," said I, expostulating, "all that was thirty years ago."

"Thirty-two years ago," she replied stiffly.

And she was right.

Mrs. Lamb presided graciously at the table, but thus far took no part in the conversation. Seated on her right, I expected that later on we would have a social chat together. But just at this, my second miscue with Miss Anderson, a mozo came into the drawing-room and spoke in Spanish to the Reverend Lamb, who seemed quite irritated. "That miserable Doña Garda," he said aloud to Mrs. Lamb, "is at the gate again."

Then in a different tone to me, "It's a woman whose boy we have taken and who now looks to us to support her and her whole family." On the sweet face of Mrs. Lamb there came a look of tenderest sympathy.

"I know you will excuse me," she said to me with winning dignity, "Doña Garda is one of my wards," and she followed the mozo from the room.

The Reverend Lamb looked vexed, and his vexation showed on all the rest except Jesus, who with obvious deference and affection, rose as Mrs. Lamb did, held the door open for her exit, and then resumed his seat.

The talk zigzagged;—whatever course it took was checked by some accuracy of Miss Anderson, and another turn soon met the same fate, but it wriggled on somehow.

There was one topic, however, on which the whole faculty, including Miss Anderson, seemed to be in thorough accord — Rome. As a reader of the *Clarion* I was, of course, familiar with Romish wickedness. Besides, I had once listened to an exposure of priestcraft by an ex-priest; the fact that the fellow was subsequently sent to the penitentiary for a gross crime gave color to the tales he told of his clerical career. But what the Reverend Lamb revealed at table that night was, nevertheless, most shocking.

" Every Mexican bandit," he said, " is regularly licensed by Rome to rob and murder, and, sir, the spoils of their crimes are duly divided with the clergy."

" Good God ! " I exclaimed, " have you proof of this ? "

"I have the testimony of one who as a priest participated in the abominable business."

" Did the scoundrel turn state's evidence ? "

" No, he turned Protestant. I myself helped to remove the scales from his eyes."

"I trust you left the ball and chain on his legs."

" No.   The reform of Brother Baez is complete. He is now earnestly coöperating in our cause."

I could feel no enthusiasm over this accession.

"And what," I asked, "is the attitude of the civil authorities toward such infamy ? "

" Civil authorities ! "   Reverend Lamb sneered. "Why, sir, one of the most prominent men in Mexico is married to his own sister. Brother Baez knows him."

"His sister ! " I exclaimed. "How was such a thing permitted ? "

"He paid the Pope $20,000 for the privi- lege," responded the Reverend Lamb, solemnly. " Brother Baez told me so."

"Every priest has a concubine," he went on. " Why, sir, some of the pupils at this Institute, Brother Baez says, are the illegitimate offspring of priests."

"Two members of my class admitted as much to me," said Miss Anderson, severely.

"I have facts," said the Reverend Lamb, impressively. "Facts of my own knowledge; facts from sources absolutely unimpeachable (I regard Brother Baez as unimpeachable); facts which, if known as I know them, would cause all Protestant Christendom —" he paused as if contemplating a sublime uprising, then closed with that peculiar lowering of his voice and brows — "to contribute to our Mission Fund."

I drew my check that night.

SEEN FROM THE ROOF

AFTER supper, the Reverend Lamb and myself repaired to the roof, where we sat and smoked, looking down on the quaint white Mexican city made glorious by the southern moon.

"What do you think of Jesus?" asked my host.

"He is a most agreeable young man. But he seems to me almost too bright for a minister — ah! — I mean to say too versatile for a missionary."

"The very quality which will make him succeed," answered the Reverend Lamb, and he went on to explain how.

"Has he accomplished any mission work as yet?" I asked.

"Indeed he has, — glorious work. His mother, whose conversion I sought for years, has at last yielded to his efforts. A week ago she was formally received into our blessed communion. We expect much from her, for, although poor, she comes of good family."

"And are you sure he will make this his life-work?"

"Not a doubt of it! Not a doubt of it! The seed planted in his soul by myself has flowered and fructified. He is to-day as ardent in the faith — "

" Yes, ardent and all that, but he is very young. Some ambition may seize him — "

" He has an ambition — a sublime ambition — to save his country from the degradation of idolatry. We created that ambition."

" But supposing he falls in love. A young fellow like that won't stay heart-whole. Whoever wins his love may rule his ambition. You cannot create his love — "

"Can't we?" The eyes of the Reverend Lamb twinkled, and a sly humor relaxed his drawn features. "Don't be too sure that we can't. Look there" — and he pointed down into the park.

I looked and saw sitting on a bench side by side, Jesus and Miss Anderson. ·

Doubtless they deemed themselves unobserved — deep shadow obscured them from the level, but to the mischievous moon and ourselves they were plainly visible.

Miss Anderson seemed to be intently studying the young man's face, while he sat with closed eyes, silent and motionless. Once she cautiously touched his hair with her forefinger, and after a

D

few such timid touches made bold to press it down as if wondering at the way it would straighten and stand. Again, I was amazed to see she placed her fingers on his pear-shaped chin and began to stroke it lovingly. His eyes snapped open. He glared upon her fierce as an animal, and clutched her in his arms. I turned to my companion. He had hastily left my side and I could just see him disappearing as he descended from the roof.

*   *   *   *   *

"They are virtually engaged," said the Reverend Lamb, apologetically, when he rejoined me.

"Engaged!"

"Not formally, you know, but we all understand it's a match."

"Why, she is old enough to be his — "

"Anchor," said the Reverend Lamb. "She will hold him to the Rock of Faith — keep him moored and safe. His marriage to her will fasten him forever to mission work."

Anchored, held, moored, and fastened forever —the words grated. Yet it was no concern of mine. So I said nothing, but the Reverend Lamb seemed to think something more ought to be said.

"A man of twenty-one," he continued, " with Spanish, Indian, and Irish blood — "

"Hot stuff!" I muttered.

" What did you remark ? "

" Not a Platonic mixture."

" Yet," said the Reverend Lamb, " he is not as ardent a lover as you might imagine."

" Possibly he is not ardently in love."

" Not in love ? After the scene we have just witnessed, can you doubt it ? "

" Well, that is by no means conclusive. One who gets heated by a stove, has not necessarily a fever ; one who sneezes from snuff, has not necessarily a cold."

" I don't quite understand," said the Reverend Lamb, coughing.

" No ! Well, you and I are old enough to be rational in such things, but, nevertheless, seat either of us with a woman, in an arbor, under a tropical moon, and let her go pawing and patting — "

I was really glad of the interruption which occurred at this point, for I could see that the train of my reflections was carrying me into a region where the Reverend Lamb might not care to accompany me.

Fortunately there was a sudden scurrying on the ladder by which we had ascended, and up darted a strange-looking bird with but one wing, pursued by a cat that had but three legs, and closely followed by an old man of dwarfed stature, whom I recognized by his scarred face and good-natured grin as the Bible Reader. Round the roof ran the bird and cat at remarkable speed considering their respective disabilities, while after them, at a pace wonderful for his age, speeded Antonio, who shouted as he went:—

"Zape, gato maldito, no molestas al pajaro! Zape, gato malo!"

Intent on his chase, he failed to see his master and myself and when at last bird and cat went in a wild whirl under our chairs, Antonio fell headlong over us.

To me the incident was amusing, and I laughed heartily. But the Reverend Lamb was greatly incensed. He rose to his feet with a remark in Spanish which, while it may have been proper enough, sounded suspiciously like an oath, and he berated the offending mozo, who stood abject and penitent before us, holding safely in his arms, however, the captured bird and cat.

"Vayase!" concluded the Reverend Lamb. "Vayase, loco, y que no vuelva a repetir semejante conducta. Vayase!"

Antonio made a bow, humble and contrite, and slunk away, talking alternately to his pets.

"I wouldn't let any of the rest off so easy,"

said Reverend Lamb, "but Antonio is a privileged character."

"Is he a brand snatched from the burning?" I asked.

"Well, hardly. He blazes every chance he gets."

This seemed so apt a repartee that it restored the Reverend Lamb's good humor, and he repeated it twice, " He blazes every chance he gets. Antonio works faithfully all week, but observes the Sabbath by getting drunk and arrested."

"Every Sabbath?"

"Every Sabbath. He is as conscientiously strict in his way of observing the day as we are in ours."

"How does Mrs. Lamb tolerate him?"

"Mrs. Lamb, like all the rest of us, is greatly attached to him. If I didn't go down to the jail every Monday morning, pay his fine and take him home, she would go herself."

"But the example, the scandal of it."

Reverend Lamb shrugged his shoulders. "This is Mexico. However it might be regarded elsewhere, nobody here gives it a thought. It is the almost universal custom of men of Antonio's class to celebrate as he does. His distinction is his absolute reliability. Faithful, competent, obliging, affectionate all week, drunk on Sunday."

"Have you tried to reform him?"

"In every way possible, even restraining him of his liberty and refusing to let him out of the yard. But to no avail. I found his Sunday spree a sanitary measure, for he got sick and useless when he was stopped. We were glad to restore him to the regular routine again."

"Has he any religion?"

"He is no papist. He has abandoned every popish practice."

"Well, we must not expect too much in one of his origin," I said.

"No!" said the Reverend Lamb. "If I could get the rest of them as far on the road to grace as Antonio —"

"As far as Antonio?"

"Yes, as far as renouncing Rome, all would be well."

"What!" I exclaimed, "is not any Christian creed better than none?"

"Rome has no Christian creed. Rome is antichrist," he answered. And for fully an hour he dwelt on this, convincing me beyond any cavil that all the ills besetting Mexico emanated from one primary evil. He only paused in his harangue that we might listen to the advanced class of Mexican girls, who (led by Miss Anderson) were singing in English the good old hymn, "I'm so glad that Jesus loves me."

CHAPTER VI

A NIGHT'S VIGIL

OTHER visits to the Institute heightened my good opinion of it. Doubtless the Reverend Lamb gave to the place its spiritual atmosphere. He had at his tongue's end, and was tireless in repeating, the most edifying scriptural passages. He was zealous in propagating the true faith, and had by far the largest number of names to his credit on the roll of converts.

Mrs. Lamb was a different type. She never quoted texts or expounded tenets; hers the broad field of charity. Besides her daily duties with the little ones, all of whom made her their confidant and loved her as a mother, she had a multitude whom she called her wards, — the poor, the sick, the lowliest of Alameda. To these she ministered, nor spared herself in season or out. " I try to help," she said, " I do not try to proselyte." Yet many with whom she worked came with her to pray; not that they knew her creed, but that they knew her goodness. Even the American residents, some of whom — invidious fellows — talked slightingly of the Reverend Lamb, making covert allusions to covetousness, one and all had words of praise for Mrs. Lamb. Her acts of charity! Her constant mission of mercy! Ay, her hero- ism! For during the fever plague, when kindred fled from kindred, she went upon her daily course from hut to hut, to rescue and relieve. Why has so little of so glorious a record appeared in the Reports or in the pages of the *Clarion?*   I cannot answer.

Gratifying also it was to find that all I saw and heard about the Institute confirmed my first im- pressions of Jesus Delancy. I found him diligent and earnest. In his classroom with his pupils he appeared particularly well. While I was unable to follow closely the language they spoke, there was no mistaking their mutual love and interest. The Reverend Lamb was an old teacher, capable and zealous, but I observed that the little ones who yawned or fidgeted under his tuition bright- ened at the entry of Jesus, and maintained an eager attention. Probably the secret of this was the young man's own enjoyment of the work. It was clearly evident that he put his heart and soul in it. Then the melody of his voice, the charm of his manner, his sensitive sympathy with every humor of the child — to all these the little sun-loved Mexicans naturally responded.

"Now you know," said the Reverend Lamb, "what I meant by the qualities that will make him signally successful as a missionary: he suits the people. He has all the good traits of his lineage, and none of the bad; for the bad, thank God, I have eradicated. There is a great career before him, — a great career."

I had come to this conclusion myself. So had Miss Anderson.

"He will be to Mexico, spiritually, what Hidalgo was politically," said she.

"Wasn't Hidalgo a priest?" I inquired.

She looked at me as if indignant at my mentioning such a thing.

"Wasn't Washington a slaveholder? Hasn't the sun spots?" she asked in her deep voice. "Hidalgo was a patriot, sir." She left the room.

"Hers is no common earthly passion for Jesus," explained the Reverend Lamb. "It is rather a pious conviction of what can be done by the union of his great talents and" — he paused before closing, with his peculiar lowering of voice and brows — "her money."

In that light, I myself was becoming reconciled to it. And day by day my interest in the lad in-

creased. The more I saw of him, the more I
liked him, and gratitude ripened liking into love.
It happened thus:—

One afternoon, it was agreed that Jesus should
call after school hours the next day, and take me
for a drive about the city; but during the night I
was taken ill with sciatica, a disease to which I am
subject, and when he came I was still in bed, suffering intensely. Did you ever have sciatica?
No? But you have had toothache. Well, they
are akin. Burns speaks of the latter as "the hell
of a' diseases"—proof that he never had the former; for if he did, he would have given sciatica
infernal supremacy. My present attack was unexpected. I had been led to believe that no such
thing could occur in the mild climate of Mexico.
Yet here it was in as violent a form as the harsh-
est winter had ever provoked at home. It seemed
as if an evil spirit with white-hot pincers pulled at
my hip, while another plied his nippers at my
heel. And there was no relief for me. A Mexican doctor whom the proprietor sent was an aggra-
vation rather than a help—a great, greasy,
bearded fellow with pudgy paws and heavy sacks
under his eyes. I put him down at once as a
quack, and would have none of his vile drugs.
How often during the long night and longer

day I wished myself back among friends and
neighbors, or anywhere in my own land among
white folks! Climate! Give me the good four
seasons, and the men and women, the fruits and
cereals, that go with them! Climate! I have seen
a consumptive friend at home waste rapidly and
die. I have seen another living and coughing in
Mexico, and telling between coughs how many
years life had been prolonged by the change, and
I have thought how much better off was he who
slept at home than he who suffered in exile.

It was when my pain was greatest, and I had
for the hundredth time become enraged at the
Mexican who attended me, and who was grossly
stupid and clumsy, that Jesus softly entered. I
did not know then that part of his missionary
training was the care of the sick, but I felt at
once something soothing in his presence. He
didn't irritate with comment or question. He was
sympathetic without speech; tender, strong. The
nourishing drink he ordered was just what I
craved, and then his deft arrangement of pillows
and bedclothes! But sciatica does not yield to
kindness or sympathy. I was still on the rack,
and groaned at every tortuous twist.

" Did you ever try massage ? " asked Jesus,
pityingly.

"Yes," I gasped; "it's a humbug."

"I often cure Miss Anderson's headaches in that way."

"Miss Anderson's headaches! O Lord!" If I were not so near crying, I could have laughed.

But an unusual wrench made me fling off the cover and clutch convulsively at my hip.

"Do let me try and help you," he pleaded, and gently laid his large warm palm upon my thigh. I felt the first touch a vital force. It thrilled my whole system. There was a peculiar shrinking ecstasy. Down the leg from hip to heel went that soft, steady, magnetic pressure. His eyes looked into mine with eager pity. The pain paused, weakened. Still shone in mine those earnest eyes and still that pulseful warmth of pressing palm! The pain vanished. I slept.

When I awoke, there came the grateful consciousness of being well. I opened my eyes and he was sitting beside me, the same intent kindliness upon his handsome face.

"Why have you not gone to supper?" I asked.

"It is time for breakfast," he answered cheerily. And it was. He had sat by me while I slept the whole night long.

CHAPTER VII

WE took our ride that afternoon, and Jesus enjoyed the outing even more than I. Indeed he was like a lad loose for a holiday. Places which soon wearied me seemed to hold him beyond reason.

We lingered long at the quaint market-place, where picturesque hucksters, men and women, boys and girls, sat or stood with their varied wares, all placidly puffing cigarettes. Here squatted a wrinkled crone, whose whole stock in trade was a hat full of corn; there an aged Indian with a pretty fawn for sale; venders of sugared stuff called "dulce," fruit, vegetables, meat, and other edibles, some on stands, some on the bare ground;—booths gay with gorgeous feather work, figures of wax, lace, saddles, and sombreros. All was orderly. Even the haggling was done with an easy, deferential courtesy. In none of the faces did I see that sharp, strained look of hungering for trade, so common in streets and marts at home. Why this universal aspect of content? Is it the climate, or is it tobacco? Or may it not be the great gift of good breeding which puts the best face on things, and forbids the outward show of inward meanness?

"All this should be familiar to you," I remarked to Jesus.

"Do you know, I have not been here since childhood," he replied almost pathetically.

"What! Were you so closely confined at the Institute?"

"It was necessary. I had to be weaned from the past. But now I can be trusted to see things as they are."

A group approached, consisting of an old man with a guitar, and his son and daughter. Stopping close to our vehicle, the aged musician struck a few chords, and the woman, who had a pleasing face and a rich contralto voice, sang: —

LA GOLONDRINA

Adonde ira veloz y fatigada
La golondrina que de aqui se va?
O, si en el aire gemira estraviada,
Buscando abrigo y no lo encontrará.
Junto a mi lecho le pondre su nido
Endonde pueda la estacion pasar;
Tambien yo estoy en la region perfida
O! Cielo santo, sin poder volar.

Dejé tambien mi patria idolotrada,
Esa mansion que me miro nacer;
　Mi vida es hoy errante y angustiada
Y ya no puedo a mi mansion volver.
　Ah! ven, querida amable perigrina,
Mi corazon al tuyo estrechare,
　Oiré tu canto, tierna golondrina,
Recordaré mi patria, y luego lloraré.

It was a song of exile — a song of love and longing for motherland. Even to me, scarce conscious of its meaning, came tender memories of home. And Jesus? His eyes closed as he listened, but one could see the emotions of the plaintive melody mirrored on his sensitive face. There was no applause; the crowd that had gathered were strangely silent. But more than one applied his blanket to moistened eyes.

When the woman went among them it was noticeable how the very poorest paid the tribute of a penny. Jesus dropped into her cup a big silver coin.

"Another song, Señorita," he pleaded.

The watchful harpist saw his unwonted fortune and with that ready tact, the wisdom of his strolling life, commenced a sweet pathetic strain. It seemed to me the daughter looked at him reproachfully, but he gave a knowing and imperative nod and again repeated the feeling prelude. With evident reluctance, she began, her voice low and trembling.

Had the old man cunningly chosen it to catch another coin from his liberal auditor? Was it for some reason too sacred with the young woman for such a purpose? I observed that all through the song, while the sharp eyes of the father were fastened on Jesus, the lowered lids of his daughter were raised not once.

It was of a youth who never had known love nor the sweets of life. But in the convent casement one day he saw a maiden fair — "una hermosa doncella, mas bella que un angel" — and their eyes gave love for love and there was no more peace for youth or maid. He pined within the prison of his home — she waned within the cruel convent walls, till death at last came in and set them free. Their souls, apart on earth, unite in heaven.

It was prettily told and soulfully sung. I looked at my companion. He was pale, tears filled his eyes.

"Let us go, Jesus," said I, but I had to take the reins myself.

Was he always so emotional? Or was it the long vigil while I slept?

During the drive he sat silent until we reached

a lofty point overlooking the city. Here we paused to contemplate a glorious picture. Beneath, lay Alameda.

Undimmed by smoke, undisfigured by chimneys, its white walls and gleaming spires clustered lovingly round nestling plazas, while everywhere the eye was charmed with countless patios of trees and flowers and fountains.

"My birthplace," said Jesus. "Is it not beautiful?"

His face lit up with loyalty and love, and in a low voice, as if to himself, he recited, rhythmically : —

ALAMEDA

Who can know and love thee not,
        Alameda.
Earth can boast no fairer spot,
        Alameda.
From afar thy temples stand,
Not as built by human hand
But as sprung from magic wand,
        Alameda.

Beauteous thou art by day,
        Alameda,
When thy sun-god holds his sway,
        Alameda ;
Yet more beauteous still by night,
Bathing in the moon's soft light,
All thy charms enchant the sight,
        Alameda.

E

"Is there no more of that?" I asked when he stopped.

He looked up smiling and blushing. "Yes, there's one more verse. But it's silly; I wrote it years ago."

"Let us have it," said I, and he continued: —

All that art has done for thee,
Alameda,
Seated on the mountain's knee,
Alameda,
Rivals not the priceless prize
That I seek with tears and sighs
In thy señorita's eyes,
Alameda.

Passing down the mountain on our way back to the city, we met a cavalcade of ladies and gentlemen, whose talk and laughter heralded their approach long before they came in sight. To my surprise, among the gay party were Nos. 1, 2, and 3 from the Institute. The gentlemen were evidently young Mexicans, and they and their horses were decked out in a fashion only seen at a circus parade. Silver and gold inlaid the saddles and glistened on their hats, jackets, and pantaloons.

"Who are those fellows?" I asked Jesus when they had passed.

"I do not know. The girls have many sweethearts, I believe," and he smiled as if it was the natural order of things. Well, probably so; but it did not accord with my former notions of missionary life. It was not the picture I had often framed in my mind at meetings of the mission board when hearing the harrowing tales of sacrifice, suffering, and hardship in the heroic fight with Rome.

But the unpleasant impression was forgotten a moment afterward when, riding along a narrow street of scattering jakals, we saw sitting in front of the meanest hut of all, Mrs. Lamb. There was a wretched, dark-featured woman beside her, whose hands she held and to whom she was talking so earnestly that our passing did not disturb her.

"That's Doña Garda," said Jesus, and added enthusiastically, "Mrs. Lamb is an angel."

Our way took us by the great cathedral famed throughout Mexico for its architectural grandeur. We drew up in front of it, and I wanted Jesus to go in with me, for I had heard much of its altars, statuary, and paintings. He declined.

"I cannot so far countenance idolatry," he said. "Just look at these benighted people!" He pointed to the interior.

We could see some distance within, where groups

were kneeling, and here and there a figure lay prostrate.

Even passers-by showed their veneration; every mozo, as he came along, would raise his hat while his lips moved in prayer.

"Is it not abominable?" said Jesus, passionately.

Now, for the life of me, I could see nothing abominable about it.

"What is the harm?" I asked.

"Why, the servility of it!" he broke forth in excitement. "Raising the hat to senseless stones!"

"But surely it is not to the stones they raise their hats. There are stones elsewhere along the streets. It is to this temple, which they believe to be the house of God."

"The day will come when Mexican manhood will scorn the practice as degrading and humiliating. All they need is familiarity with the true faith."

"Well, here comes one familiar with the true faith," said I.

It was Antonio. With a bundle under each arm, he was speeding from the market homeward. He did not notice us, such was his hurry, yet, when he got to the church, he halted, put down the bundles, raised his hat devoutly, then resuming his burden, started off on his peculiar trot.

I could not help laughing at the chagrin of Jesus.

"Antonio is incorrigible," he said, "but there are others — "

And there were. Even as he spoke, his eyes caught the outline of a woman's figure emerging from the gloom of the interior, and he paused. I observed his strained look, and following its direction saw the woman reverently dip her finger in the holy-water font, bless herself, and come out. As she was about to pass, she raised her eyes and an expression of recognition at once and shame came over her worn features. She hesitated, trembling, troubled, then stood with extended arms.

"Jesus! hijo mio!" she murmured.

The look of pain and deep resentment in the face of Jesus changed instantly to one of love, and leaping out he embraced his mother.

I stole away into the church so as to leave them for a space together. When I came back, Jesus was alone, and his eyes met mine with an infinite sadness and pride.

From the church we turned into a business thoroughfare. To an American whose idea of Mexico is a confusion of adobe and cactus, and whose ideal Mexican is a slouching, ear-ringed fellow with blanket and sombrero, such a street is a revelation. Massive structures of brick and stone, banks, office buildings, telegraph and telephone, street cars, omnibuses, hacks and all kinds of modern vehicles, well-dressed men, and ladies elegant in the latest Paris fashions, bustling clerks and hustling porters—everywhere the alert aspect of trade and the rush and war of active traffic. One could easily have thought himself in some thriving city of the North. As I looked, the great bell of the cathedral sounded three solemn strokes. A hush fell upon the throng. Hats were raised, heads bowed, and knees bent. The bell had announced the Ave Maria.

CHAPTER VIII

THE STUBBY MAN

WE supped together at the hotel. We were to conclude the day's outing by going to the plaza for the usual Thursday evening concert and promenade. Jesus was singularly reserved, almost melancholy. Failing in every effort to rouse him to his accustomed cheerfulness, I became interested in the various groups about the dining room. Without exception, they were noticeable for loud talk and violent gesture. It is said that there are but two places at which the Mexican lets himself loose — the restaurant and the bull-ring. Not having at that time ever seen a bull-fight, I could not speak for their conduct there, but surely more cackling and shouting and all-around coarseness were displayed in that dining room than I had yet seen elsewhere in Mexico.

"Your countrymen are rather noisy at meals," I remarked to Jesus.

"And yours seem, if anything, noisier."

The reply was so unlike him, I looked up in surprise. He nodded moodily toward a party of gentlemen who occupied an adjoining table and were particularly garrulous and demonstrative. Sure enough, they were Americans, five of them, and four of the five were talking away at once as vociferous as auctioneers. It was impossible to tell from their clamor what they were talking about. But at the height of the din an obstinate cork with which their waiter had been struggling went off with a resonant pop, and there was sudden silence. Forgetting · their contention, all watched critically the filling of the glasses, after draining which the rival tongues again ran riot until another pop made peace.

The fifth member of the group had taken no part in the previous wrangle. He seemed content to listen and drink, and he did both with grim deliberation. But, after the second bottle, he spoke, and the rest were respectfully and unexpectedly silent. He was a short, stout, reddish-faced man, who can be best described by the word "stubby." In a multitude of ways he suggested that term. His hair was stubby, his beard ditto, ears, nose, body, hands, and feet all stubby. It seemed as if he had originally started out to be big, and suddenly stopped short. Even his voice gave the same impression. It was strong, but abrupt.

"Idiot," he spoke, "spends week Texas, or

shoots in and out of the country by rail, thinks write book Mexico." Each word was a growl.

"But Prescott's history says—" began one of the party.

"Stuff!" harshly interrupted the stubby man.

"Well, Wallace's 'Fair God'—" remarked another.

"Rot!" snarled the stubby man and went on: "Takes years know man. How long take know people? I'm here fifteen years. In fifteen more, may—" here he stopped abruptly and drained his glass.

"Write a book?" questioned one.

But he vouchsafed no reply.

"There's a sensible man," said Jesus.

"I thought," modestly ventured another of the party, "the cruelty of the Spaniards to the natives was undisputed."

"Of course, undisputed. Why not?" snapped the stubby man. "So cruelty Normans Saxons, British Irish, cruelty all conquerors conquered. What our treatment natives?"

"Oh! Our Indians are nearly all—"

"Dead!" growled the stubby man. "Yes! Dead while Indians Mexico survive. Eight millions of them. We killed ours off and have damned impudence"— he stopped and drank again —"to send missionaries to Mexico."

Jesus was listening with a look of pleased approval, but at the closing words his face clouded.

The stubby man said no more, and his companions, who for some reason seemed awed by him, were soon babbling away again.

"Do you know," shouted one, "the beauty of Alameda will be on the plaza to-night."

"Who is she?"

"Why, the daughter of Governor Romero."

"She is a beauty," said another, "but she is engaged to Licenciado Francisco Benavides."

"Did you hear that name?" Jesus inquired of me.

"Benavides?"

"No. Governor Romero. My grandfather saved his life once."

"Indeed! How was that?"

"By refusing to fight a duel with him."

I had to laugh at the seriousness with which he gave the reply. He assured me, however, that a duel with his grandfather was no laughing matter. And, as he walked from the dining room and I observed his splendid height, massive shoulders, and easy, supple carriage, I could not help thinking he was right, if the grandfather bore much resemblance to the grandson.

CHAPTER IX

THE ARREST

WE strolled down to the plaza. It was my first
view of a scene that I had often read and heard
of. Round a public square, glorious with tropical trees and plants and playing fountains that
gleamed and shimmered in the fierce stare of
electric lamps and the mellow glow of the moon,
there promenaded to the music of a magnificent
band several thousand people, ladies in one column, gentlemen in the other, moving in opposite
directions. For some minutes we stood watching
the circling multitude, then we joined the male
procession and, arm in arm, went the rounds.

Young people in Mexico are not permitted the
same freedom as with us. Cupid must shoot at
long range. Ante-nuptial intimacy is forbidden.
But this romantic countermarching on the plaza
takes its place. Face to face at every round, El
Señor meets La Señorita; at every round, answering eyes make love. Now chance is found to
fling a kiss — now notes are swiftly passed — love,

that laughs at locksmiths and outwits the wisest
the world over, finds here his ways and means of
courtship.

It did not take long to tire me tramping round,
but I believe Jesus would have walked that plaza
forever. "Just one more turn," he would plead to
my protest of weariness, and after that again and
again, "one more."

We seated ourselves at last on a bench where I
thought we could observe all the rest. Unfortunately the noisy group of Americans who occupied
the adjoining table at tea were on the same bench
and loud as ever. Nothing more mars one's
enjoyment of a thing of beauty than vapid babble.
Their pointless jibes and jokes became intolerable.
I wondered how the stubby man, who sat with
them, endured it. "Let us leave," I whispered,
standing up; and my companion rose reluctantly.
At this moment one of the loud young men called
out: "Look, boys! There comes the Governor
and his daughter."

A carriage was driving up, in which were
seated a very old gentleman and a very young
lady. The carriage stopped almost beside us,
and, as much to make room for the occupants to
alight as out of curiosity, we resumed our seats.
The Governor, for it was he, dignifiedly handed

out his daughter, and she passed so close that I had a good view of her face. Now I have reached the age when we become critical and discriminating in the matter of female beauty. I can reason whether it is a gift of nature or a work of art, how much of it is due to the setting, how much is subjective, — an age when, in fact, I supposed myself free from prejudice or passion and incapable of surprise. But the face of Señorita Romero dazzled me; she was a goddess aglow with the glory of her own loveliness. Describe her! I have tried to do so again and again, and failed flatly. As well describe the blossom or the sunbeam — perfume or music.

"Well, I declare," said I, turning to Jesus, "that is the most perfect — " But the expression of his face stopped me. I had seen in the church that afternoon just such a look on an Indian girl, standing with clasped hands before a statue of the virgin.

"Don't last, these señoritas," came the rasping voice of the stubby man. "Early ripe, early rot."

Jesus didn't hear, nor did he move.

Soon the Governor and his daughter made the round and passed again. She was chatting gayly, and her voice, sweet and soft, was in harmony

with her face.   Now, I had seen all I came to see,
and it was my usual time for retiring, yet there
we sat another hour, and for what? — just to
catch, every few minutes, a glimpse of a pretty
girl; and throughout that hour, explain it if you
can, neither missionary nor graybeard spoke a
word.

At last the Governor, as he approached, waved
his hand to the watchful coachman and escorted
his daughter toward the carriage.   The cochero
leaped from his box to open the carriage door.
In doing so, the reins were awkwardly flung on
the horses' haunches, and the startled animals
plunged violently.   Two or three little policemen
sprang at their heads, but only increased their
fright, and they reared and backed the carriage
on the curbing.   The excited Governor left his
daughter's side, and giving confused orders in
Spanish, tried to seize the reins.   In the effort
his foot slipped, and he fell under the horses'
hoofs.

"Mi Padre!   Salvenlo!" shrieked his daughter.

With a bound Jesus clutched him by the collar
and jerked him to safety, but so forcibly, it
seemed to me the old man's neck snapped, then
springing to the horses' heads, soon mastered
them.   There was a chorus of vivas from the

crowd, and the Señorita beamed her gratitude. Not so the Governor. He had not realized his danger. He deemed himself assaulted. It took him some time to get breath, but when he did his eyes were bulging and his face purple. "Bribon atrevido!" he cried, shaking his fist at Jesus. "Vd. me ha asaltado." Then turning to the police who had gathered, he shouted: —

"Aresten a este hombre! Arestenlo!"

At this order to arrest, a little bow-legged fellow, eager to show his prowess before the Governor, rushed upon Jesus, clutched his throat, and strove to push him backward. For a moment, Jesus was too astonished to resist; but only for a moment. Flinging off his assailant as he would a fly, he drew himself to his lordly height and cast on the Governor a look of leonine indignation and defiance. I tried to interpose and explain, but my efforts only redoubled the Governor's rage.

"Arestenlo! Soy el Gobernador;" he repeated. "Arestenlo!"

Fully a dozen officers now started for Jesus, some of them with hands on pistols.

"Yield, Delaney!" I cried. "Yield, man, we can explain."

"Yield! I will die first!" There was an ugly

curl of the lip and a glare in the eyes that was ferocious. Every savage instinct was aroused. His mighty arm shot out, and down went a policeman. Right and left he struck as they advanced, and every blow felled an adversary. With nature's weapons, he was match for a multitude. But pistols were drawn. I saw the gleam and heard the click.

"Good God! What an outrage!" I shouted, and forgetting my years and infirmities, brought my cane down on the head of a scoundrel who was about to shoot.

"I'm with you, old boy!" growled the stubby man at my side, and he smote a Philistine on the skull. Just then, I saw a dastardly deed. A tall, swarthy man with white, prominent teeth, came from the crowd that was watching the fray, and sneaking behind Jesus, felled him with a fearful blow from a heavy cane. The officers pounced on the fallen man. The battle was over.

In vain Señorita Romero cast her arms round her father's neck and pleaded. His dignity had to be vindicated. The prisoner was carted away. I saw an officer point at me as if suggesting my active complicity. But the Governor shook his head; he was satiated with a single victim. I was bewildered, the whole occurrence was so sudden, senseless, terrific. I looked about for the stubby man. He was gone. The band was playing another march, and the crowd that had gathered melted again into the double procession.

F

CHAPTER X

IT was some time before I could control myself sufficiently to decide what should be done. Then I summoned a hack and ordered the driver to carry me to the city prison. We drew up before an imposing structure, at whose doors soldiers stood on guard. Entering the dingy office, I asked a fat man who sat at a desk if I could see my friend. He did not even deign to look at me as he gruffly replied : —

"No! Esta incomunicado."

It is the custom, I was afterward informed, to keep persons arrested on a criminal charge inaccessible for three days to any one except the criminal judge. During such a period the accused is " incomunicado."

I asked if he knew the extent of his injuries; he shrugged his shoulders.

"But he is injured. Can I not send him a doctor ? "

"No! Esta incomunicado."

I insisted that there must be some way of securing for the prisoner proper medical attendance. Again that dubious shrug. Disheartened, I turned from the uncommunicative brute and walked out. A respectable-looking man followed me.

"I can tell you, sir, how you can have a physician see your friend," he said in very good English.

"You will greatly oblige me by doing so."

"I myself am a physician, and I think with a little money I can gain admittance to the prisoner," he answered, handing me his card. It read:—

DOCTOR RAFAEL MEDINA,

MEDICO-CIRUJANO

De la Facultad de Mexico

I eyed him closely, for I am not one to be easily imposed upon.

His clean-shaven face, plain black clothes, and solemn expression gave him an appearance decidedly clerical. But his eyes were convincing. If ever eyes were windows of the soul, such seemed to be the eyes of Doctor Medina. A soul looked out from them,—a soul full of tenderness, truthfulness, and intelligence, an honest soul, a good soul. My doubts vanished.

" How much money will it take ? "

" About ten dollars," he replied with a frank smile.

" Will five do ? " I asked, desirous of making as good a bargain as possible.

" It may," said he, dubiously; then brightening up resolutely — " It must " — he added.

" Then here is five dollars.   The prisoner's name is Jesus Delaney.   He has a wound on the back of his head.   Attend him and report to me at the Hotel San José to-night."   I drove to the Institute.

I was glad to see a light there, for it was already late.   I rapped at the heavy oaken door with my cane.

"Who is there ? "   It was the voice of Miss Anderson.

" Me ! "

" Me ! "   The pronoun was protested.   " Who are you, sir ? "

My name gained me admittance.

" Is the Reverend Lamb still up ? "

" No !   He has retired."   She was grim and suspicious.

" What is the trouble ? "

I hesitated.   A woman and the affianced of the unfortunate man — could she bear the shock ?

Her calm demeanor decided me. Gently, delicately as possible, I broke the news. She never winced. It was I who was nervous. Several times during the narration she interrupted to correct names and details of no earthly moment, and at the close I had the uncomfortable feeling of a schoolboy who has just made a most discreditable recitation.

"What business had you and he on the plaza?" she asked severely.

"Just curiosity."

"Curiosity," with profound reproof, "the sin of Adam."

"Going there was my fault entirely, Miss Anderson, not his."

"It was unbecoming in both. He is a missionary, you an old man."

This nettled me. I felt like retorting that even to be old and a missionary at the same time did not save some people from folly; but I checked myself and respectfully requested her to call the Reverend Lamb.

"I doubt the propriety, sir," she said, "of disturbing him on any such business."

"Why, madam, his assistant is in a Mexican bastile, and he is — "

"There is no bastile in Mexico," she interrupted, accenting bastile on the last syllable. "It existed

in France until 1789, when it was destroyed during
the Revolution."

"In a lousy lock-up, then, madam, and he's
wounded!" I was downright angry with her.

"Wounded!" There was a perceptible tremor
in the tone, but she managed to emphasize a pronunciation differing from mine.

"Yes! Wounded and bloody. A scoundrel
smashed him on the head—" I said no more, for
Miss Anderson, with uplifted hands, whimpered
weakly, "O dear! I will call Brother Lamb,"
and left the room.

I expected that the Reverend Lamb would be
deeply grieved and shocked, but he wasn't. On
the contrary, as I related the affair, there came
upon his face an expression of positive gratification. He must have observed my surprise at this,
for when his eyes caught mine, a quick, conscious
change came on him. "Ah! It is too bad! Too
bad!" he remarked, but he didn't look as if it was
particularly bad—in fact there appeared to be
something particularly good in it, for he assumed
the forlorn with evident effort.

"What is to be done?" I asked.

"Nothing can be done to-night."

"What! Must we leave him in jail like a felon?
Is there no bail, no habeas corpus for such a case?"

" There is the will of Governor Romero," he answered complacently. " He is the accuser, the law, and the court."

" Damn such a country ! "

" Brother ! "

" Damn such a country ! " I repeated, and went off without saying good night.

But in the hall I met Mrs. Lamb, to whom I had to relate what happened. She was much moved : indeed, when I came to tell how Jesus had been stricken down and jailed, she seemed about to faint, and I ran for water to the room in which I had left the Reverend Lamb. Hastily entering, I was amazed to see him standing looking up at the ceiling with the broadest kind of a grin on his face.

" Your wife is ill," I exclaimed, and seizing the pitcher rushed back.

He came after me showing much concern, but we found Mrs. Lamb recovered.

" Jesus must be released at once," she said; " what a gross outrage on our boy ! "

" Nothing can be done now," said the Reverend Lamb, meekly. " But I will report the outrage to the Board. It will cause great indignation and much sympathy for the cause — much sympathy." Something like a satisfied smirk flitted over his otherwise solemn countenance.

Mrs. Lamb's cheeks flushed and her eyes blazed on her husband as she said, "The report can wait, but Jesus must not be allowed to lie in that jail. If you don't act, then I will — "

"We will act in the morning, be assured," said he, more meekly still.

With this assurance I left, and on my way to the hotel kept wondering how the Reverend Lamb ever won so magnificent a woman.

CHAPTER XI

THE Reverend Lamb was at my room early the next morning. He seemed to have reached the conclusion during the night that it was his duty to take prompt measures for the release of Jesus. He was earnest, resolute, and urgent, in marked contrast to his manner of the evening previous, making the latter all the more inexplicable.

"We must see the American consul," he said. "Consul Leech is intimate with the Governor and is a friend of mine. I know he will assist us."

I wondered why he hadn't suggested this course when I first spoke to him, but there was no time to lose in questioning. Off we started to the American consulate. It was not yet open.

"We will go to his residence," said the Reverend Lamb, and there we went. The consul was in the garden, but came as soon as we were announced. I had heard a good deal of Consul Leech. He was often mentioned in the press as an efficient officer, watchful of American interests, and was

frequently referred to in the *Mission Clarion* as
a good friend of the cause, so I had formed a
most favorable opinion of him. But his appearance, as he came in, was disappointing. Not
because he wore a dirty pair of overalls and was
barefooted — he explained that by his occupation
— but a humorless smile, or rather grin, which he
carried constantly, and a sort of uneasy, ferrety
look in his eyes, gave me an uncomfortable sense
of craft and meanness. My first impressions,
however, are often wrong — very often, and I am,
on that account, disposed to distrust them.

He was above the average in height and weight,
had coarse, straight, sandy hair, thin, faded chin
whiskers somewhat frosted, and that tallowy skin
which is ever fertile of freckles. He was not
well-mannered. He lacked dignity and made
too apparent a certain self-conscious assumption
of good fellowship.

During my relation of the occurrence on the
plaza he kept grinning and nodding his head
wisely, and commenting with "Ah!" "Yes!" or
"O!" at every sentence, but when he looked at
me at all, it was furtively.

"And now, Consul, we want your aid," said the
Reverend Lamb, as I finished.

"Ah! Yes! Of course," he replied; "but

is Mr. — ah! I mean — Reverend Delaney — an American?" He spoke with a nasal twang, at times drawling his words and again hurrying them, while he never ceased to grin.

"No. He is a Mexican."

"Then — ah! — why — it is no affair of mine — that is — ah — officially."

"But can you not help us?"

"Ah! Yes! Of course, but — you see — not officially — " he paused and grinned us over composedly, then went on — "If you wish to engage my services — ah — of course," he grinned constantly — in fact leered, it seemed to me.

Now I abominate indirection; I like a man to plump out what he means.

"Do you mean, Mr. Consul, that you are ready to be employed in this matter?" I asked bluntly.

"Well, you see — ah — as an attorney and all that (he grinned and drawled) I am entitled — "

"To compensation. How much will it cost?" I interrupted.

"Ah! Let me see." He stopped grinning, drew a piece of paper, knitted his brow, and began computation. This was evidently congenial work. He no longer posed. It was the chance of an artist to catch the dominant character of a face that never suggested the image and likeness of

Him who said, "Thou shalt not covet thy neighbor's goods."

"Well," he said at last, "you had best have your statement drawn up formally. This I will present to the Governor. Then I will make my argument and — well — I can't state the exact cost, but let us say twenty dollars down and the balance, whatever it may be — " he was regaining his grin.

"But please name a maximum, sir. I don't want to incur expense blindly."

"Well," and he scanned me out of his small eyes as if to see how much I would bear, "it may reach fifty dollars."

"I am willing to pay fifty dollars to secure that young man's release," I said.

Leech at work was prompt and methodical. He took down my statement in English, which he requested the Reverend Lamb to translate into Spanish, and in less than an hour had it signed and sealed and was ready to set out for the Governor's.

"I will call at your hotel as soon as I have definite news," he said. I paid him twenty dollars in advance and promised the balance immediately on my friend's release. The Reverend Lamb and myself then proceeded to the jail. On our way we met four policemen, three of whom had badly battered faces, and the fourth a bandaged head. The latter eyed me suspiciously, and I have a notion he was the one I gave the clip with my cane.

Reverend Lamb's mastery of Spanish gave him a more voluble audience with the obese brute behind the desk, but the result was the same. Jesus was "incomunicado." Nobody could see him but the criminal judge.

" Had that officer yet appeared?"

" No!"

" When would he?"

A shrug.

" How long would the incommunication last?"

"Seventy-two hours."

" After that, could we see him?"

" Quien sabe," with a shrug.

We departed, going to the hotel, where we waited for Leech, who came within an hour. He was smirking as one thoroughly satisfied with himself.

"Good news," he said; "I have arranged an audience with the Governor at two."

" Is that all?" I was disappointed.

"Ah!" he grinned, "you cannot hurry things in Mexico."

"But the man is in jail and wounded — the victim of a gross outrage."

" Ah! yes," and he grinned, "his misfortune."

We could neither see the prisoner, nor get any satisfactory account of him. There was nothing to be done.

I accompanied the Reverend Lamb to the Institute. Miss Anderson met us at the door with a judicial cast of countenance.

"Well ? " she inquired, and in her deep voice there was condemnation and command. It made me feel cheap and culpable.

"We have no news," I said humbly, "but" (I tried to be cheerful) " you know no news is good news."

"I know no such thing, sir !" My cheerfulness congealed.

"We have done all we could."

" And accomplished nothing ? "

" Nothing," I confessed.

"Brother Lamb," she said tragically, "have I your permission to act in this disgraceful affair ? "

"Oh, certainly! Certainly, Miss Anderson. Any help you can give us — "

" I don't seek to be your auxiliary, sir. I wish to move personally and independently," and giving him and me a scathing glance, she left.

"And you tell me Jesus is to marry that woman?" I asked the Reverend Lamb.

"Yes."

"God help him!"

He did not say Amen, but he really looked it.

Late in the afternoon, Leech put in an appearance, grinning.

"Did you see the Governor?"

"No, not yet, but —"

"Then nothing has been done?" I was disgusted.

"I have arranged to see his Excellency at ten o'clock to-morrow morning."

"And no way of reaching the prisoner until then?"

"No. He is incomunicado. The matter — ah — is very serious," he repeated. "I would advise you to retain a good lawyer — one of influence — say — ah — Licenciado Francisco Benavides. He is the Governor's prospective son-in-law."

"I authorize you to retain him," said I, promptly, for I had concluded, with Leech, that the affair was indeed serious.

CHAPTER XII

POOR LUPITA

AMERICANS have not the language faculty — at least, they are slow to learn Spanish. I have met them ignorant of the language after a residence in Mexico of twenty years. I have met them born and raised on the border and among Spanish-speaking people all their lives, without acquiring it. And it is a curious fact that Mexicans seem equally inapt in learning English. Not so, however, other foreigners. Germans, French, and Jews particularly are natural linguists. The average German picks up Spanish in a few months; the average Jew in a few days.

So, it is not to be wondered at that Miss Anderson, after her long residence in Alameda, could not speak it fluently. But this did not deter her from setting out in her own way to accomplish the release of Jesus.

She reasoned that if the facts were as stated by the Reverend Lamb and myself, all that was necessary was to place them properly before the authorities. And this she made up her mind to do. What she did and what came of it I will here set down, for the facts all reached me in time.

Taking along as her interpreter, Lupita, a bright little pupil of the Institute, thirteen years old, with the fresh pretty face of a child and the plump rounded figure of a woman, Miss Anderson went to the jail.

Here the Fat Official imparted the same information as he had vouchsafed to the Reverend Lamb and me. And far from being rude or reticent as with us, he was so very deferential, so very considerate, so very profuse in his offers of aid, in his protestations of sympathy, that Miss Anderson was not only satisfied Jesus was "incomunicado," she was actually convinced that he was properly so, and that it was a piece of great good fortune that he was under the kindly care of one so eminently courteous and obliging. If such was the influence of the Fat Official on Miss Anderson, deeper and stronger was the impression he made on Lupita, who was the interpreter through whom his gracious words were spoken. For, while conveying all the assurances mentioned regarding the condition of Jesus and his own good intentions, he managed to beam on the little one a gracious, unctuous, melting admiration, such as she had never known or dreamt of. "Que hermosa!" (How beautiful!) he would sigh at the end of a sentence, while his big eyes stuck out of baggy sockets. "Hermosisima!" he would murmur, until Lupita's face shone like burnished bronze. No wonder little Lupita willingly prolonged the interview! No wonder she reluctantly followed her teacher from the jail! No wonder that, as she went, she looked back to drink again the fervor of those big eyes and thrill with kisses thrown from fat lips by flabby hands.

It was full three squares on her way homeward before Miss Anderson recovered from the Fat Official's spell and bethought her of the utter failure of her mission. Jesus was still in jail. She had done nothing, learned nothing, was simply inthralled by the charming manners of an underling. It must not be. She would try the Governor himself.

To the office of his Excellency she went with Lupita. "He is engaged," said the secretary.

"I will wait," responded Miss Anderson, and sat determinedly down.

"He may be engaged all day," said the secretary.

"Tell him I will wait all day," said Miss Anderson, and Lupita so informed him.

What a weazened wretch that secretary was! With pen in mouth, bending over his work, how much he resembled some bird of prey! Thus thought Lupita, and her mind wandered back to another face and form, oh, so different, and her eye wandered to the door they had just entered, and retraced the way they had just come until — yes — there, beaming, melting, overflowing still with admiration, stood the Fat Official. And was it to be wondered if Lupita started, reddened, smiled — ay, threw back with her little hand the kiss thrown to her, while Miss Anderson firmly sat unconscious of it all?

Presently the door of an inner office opened. The alert secretary flew forward. There was a short conference and the secretary announced " El Gobernador."

Suave, stately, benign, Governor Romero approached Miss Anderson. If the Fat Official heard her with considerate attention, if she was charmed by the kindness and sympathy there, what must have been her experience with the Governor — the most gracious, well-bred, polished gentleman in Alameda? Miss Anderson left the executive office in a grateful glow of belief that it was only the forbearance, the beneficent kindliness of his Excellency that saved Jesus from the extreme rigor of the law.

But disenchantment was again rapid. Before reaching the Institute, she was face to face once more with the cold fact of failure. She had sneered at Reverend Lamb and me, and here was herself put off with nice palaver. It must not be. Yet another way was open. She had enough of Mexican men — she would now try Mexican women. And off she started for the Governor's residence.

Ordinarily, it would have been no easy matter to gain access to Madam or Miss Romero, but there are times in all Republics when even the families of public men are accessible, and fortunately for Miss Anderson this was such a time. She was received by both ladies with marked kindness. She was listened to not with mere courtesy — there was a real sympathetic interest in the anxiety of the old lady and the tears of the young.

"Hija, debemos libertar ese joven caballero," said Madam Romero.

"Este Vd. segura, querida señora, que su joven amigo sera pronto en libertad. Yo se lo prometo."

It was the assurance of success, the proffer and promise of liberty for Jesus. Miss Anderson went away in triumph.

She was so much taken up with rejoicing, she did not notice the Fat Official standing at the door as she came out, or that he followed down the street, or that he was near when she stopped at a corner to watch a military band go proudly by. How gay their plumes! How glorious their music! It did Miss Anderson good to see and hear. But when the band had floated away in a sea of sound and color far down the street and she turned to take Lupita's hand, Lupita was gone.

Up and down searched Miss Anderson, here, there, everywhere, no Lupita. Doubtless the child had followed the music and was lost.

*   *   *   *   *

At ten o'clock that night, Lupita returned to the Institute. At the same hour, the Fat Official reappeared at his desk. Poor Lupita!

CHAPTER XIII

THE CHALLENGE

IT was the third day after the arrest of Jesus. We had not yet succeeded in seeing or hearing from him. Regularly morning and afternoon I called at the consular office. Leech had the same story, a coming audience with the Governor. The Mexican lawyer, Licenciado Benavides, was engaged, he said, but even he could do nothing professionally until the period of incomunicado had expired.

"Nothing professional," Leech would repeat and grin meaningly. "But I have great hopes of his influence with the Governor."

It was arranged that on the evening of the third day we should have a consultation, — Leech, Benavides, the Reverend Lamb, and myself.

I walked over to the consulate at the appointed hour, and found Leech and the Reverend Lamb already there. We waited full two hours for Benavides.

"It is the Mexican way," explained Leech.

At last the door opened and there entered a tall, swarthy man with prominent teeth, whom I recognized instantly as the villain who had struck Jesus. I arose, clutching my cane.

"This is Señor Licenciado Francisco Benavides," said Leech, pompously. The Mexican raised his hat, bowed courteously, and held forth his hand. I looked him straight in the eye and, ignoring the proffered hand, spoke out: "I know this fellow. He is the sneak who struck down Jesus Delaney. I refuse his acquaintance."

Knowing that I could not restrain myself further, I bowed to Leech and Lamb and left the office.

The Reverend Lamb came running after me. He was pale and excited.

"You know not what you have done. Benavides is the Governor's closest adviser, and will be his son-in-law."

"I don't give a damn if he was the President. He is a dirty dog," I said fiercely.

I record this unbecoming language with deep regret and offer as apology the indignation that had smouldered in my mind since witnessing the cowardly assault. It was so unmanly, so treacherous — I fired into flame at thought of it.

Just then, up came Leech. He had lost his grin and seemed frightened.

"You must apologize," he gasped.   "You must apologize!"

"Apologize!   You, the American consul, ask me to apologize to such a cur!"   He backed away from me. I could have flogged him. It was mean enough in the preacher, but a consul!

"I see neither of you have the instincts of a gentleman," I said. "Good evening," and I walked from them to my hotel. Indignation doubtless had the better of me, that was plain. But the damage was done. I went to my room and tried to think the matter over.   What would come of it?   How would it affect Jesus?

There was a rap at the door and a boy entered, bearing this card:—

RAMON SANCHEZ ALATORRE

GENERAL DE BRIGADA

Who could the party be?   What did he want?
"Show him up," I said to the boy.
"Que?"
"Show him up!"
"Que?"
"O! diga la hombre — to — that is — passe in my room — I mean — in my cuarto — confound the language."

The boy understood. In a moment I heard a heavy step ascending the stair, and soon a sharp knock.

"Come in," I shouted.

Another knock.

"Ah! Passe! Passe!"

The door opened and there entered a stout, elderly man of a complexion dark as a negro, wearing a red-lined military cloak, and of elaborate military bearing. He bowed ceremoniously and I motioned him to a chair. But he remained standing.

"Soy el General Sanchez Alatorre, del Ejercito Mexicano," he said, speaking slowly and distinctly, just the way I like to hear Spanish spoken. He was General Alatorre of the Mexican army.

I bowed.

"Vengo, Señor, como el amigo del Licenciado Don Francisco Benavides, y como su enviado especial en un asunto quizas desagradable." For the first time in Mexico, I understood every word that was spoken. He had come as the friend of Benavides.

I bowed again.

"Mi mision es de exigir de Vd. escusas y completa satisfacion por insultos de que, con razon, se queja mi principal."

"Ah! He wants satisfaction, does he? Wants an apology? Say to your friend, sir—"

"No entiendo, Señor," he interrupted. He did not understand me.

"Diga to your amigo—diga al Señor—he can—puede go to the devil!" I was off again, mad as a hornet.

"Que dice Vd., Señor, no entiendo."

"Diga al Señor, I will see him in hell first."

"Dispense Vd., Señor, no entiendo lo que Vd. me dice."

There was a stately courtesy about the old gentleman as he declared his inability to understand me that must have contrasted with my ill temper and undignified demeanor.

"Diga al Señor Benavides que no apologize, no doy satisfacion—not by a damned sight." He understood.

"Entonces, Señor, en nombre del Licenciado Benavides, tengo el honor de presentar a Vd. esta communicacion. Buenas noches, Caballero," and handing me a sealed letter, he bowed himself out. Breaking the seal, I read the following:—

SEÑOR: Hoy, en el Consulado Americano, sin causa y sin razon, tuvo Vd. la temeridad de dirijirme un insulto lastimando gravemente mi amor propio y mi honor de caballero.

Altamente ofendido por tan rudo e indigno proceder, he

comisionado a mi amigo el General Sanchez Alatorre para
que, en mi representacion, exige de Vd. una satisfacion ade-
cuada a la ofensa.

En caso contrario (que no es de esperarse) puede Vd.
mandar sus representantes a mis padrinos, Sres. General
Sanchez Alatorre y Coronel Joaquin Zuluaga, quienes se
ponen a sus ordenes en la Comandancia Militar, Avenida
Juarez, No. 15.

> Soy de Vd. Sr. el atento servidor,
> LICENCIADO FRANCISCO BENAVIDES.

I had no trouble in translating it. It was a challenge to a duel.

CHAPTER XIV

THE ACCEPTANCE

I, who had been all my life a law-abiding citizen and for years President of our Humane Society, challenged to fight a duel! It was absurd, and I laughed; but it was nevertheless a fact. What should I do? Accept? Out of the question. Tear the challenge and go about my business? That was the simplest solution — certainly the only proper course for a man of my character and conscience. "But if I do so," I reasoned, "what will that miserable creature think? Doubtless that I am afraid of him. Afraid of a wretch who sneaked behind a man already beset by a mob, and struck him down? He takes this way of making a reputation for courage, challenging a man of sixty! He doesn't know that where I came from men are as well preserved at sixty as the average weazened Mexican at forty. I have a mind to show him that age doesn't unmake a man. Besides, such a fellow won't dare fight." But of this last I wasn't so sure. I recalled the case of one Ed. Rogers at home who was known to be afraid of his own shadow, and didn't resent the pulling of his nose, yet turned out a very dare-devil on the battle-field. This Benavides might be such another — a poltroon in a brawl, desperate in a duel. Courage is an unknown quantity till tested. Thus I talked and argued with myself, growing more and more irresolute. It occurred to me at last to take counsel in the matter. But with whom? Not Leech, whining, white-livered Leech. Not Lamb. It was no affair for a minister. Disturbed and undecided, I went downstairs into the lobby of the hotel. No face inviting confidence was visible. The bushy-haired clerk behind the desk, the bushy-haired porter perched on his stand, were the only occupants of the office. I walked to the entrance, and there, by himself, sat the Stubby Man.

How an emergency makes friends! I did not know the man's name, had never exchanged a word with him, yet his action at that crisis on the plaza made him seem a comrade. We shook hands and I seated myself beside him.

"I did not see you after the fracas the other night," I said, smiling.

He nodded.

"I want to thank you for standing by me."

Another nod.

I waited for some remark, but he was grimly silent.

"Have you lived long in Mexico?" I asked.

"Years." Another long pause.

"Do you know anything about their duelling customs here?"

"All."

"Did you ever fight a duel yourself?"

"Three."

"Were they serious?"

A shrug. Everybody in Mexico has that shrug; natives by instinct, others by example. You don't like it at first. But you get used to it and in time acquire it as an important factor in conversation. Only the Mexican, however, has an easy, natural mastery of all its varied meanings.

"Were you ever injured?" I asked.

"No!"

"O! Your opponents were —"

"Winged," he paused. "Lamed," a longer pause. "Pinked," I thought he was through, but after some time he grunted, "respectively."

Despite his reticence and jerky speech, he impressed me as a man of good sense. Besides, his conduct on the plaza bore testimony to his courage and loyalty. Why not confide in him? On the impulse of the moment, I so decided and handed him the challenge.

He read and returned it without remark. I told him the whole story. But in vain did I wait for some comment. His set face showed neither sympathy nor interest. It was discouraging.

"What had I best do?" I finally asked.

"'Cept," he answered promptly.

"But I am opposed on principle to duelling."

"Apologize."

"Damned if I will!"

"Skip!"

"If you mean that I should leave this place —"

"Country," he grunted.

"Leave the country," I continued; "I want to say that I am an American citizen, have my passport as such, and am entitled to the protection of the law."

"Law!" he snorted.

"Is there no law here?"

A shrug.

"Well, sir, I will remain here and test that."

I arose and walked up and down, keeping time, time, time to three words that crowded all else from my mind and forced themselves upon me pitilessly: Accept, apologize, skip! Accept, apologize, skip!

Passion said accept, reason said skip, but let me here assert not once did any craven instinct urge apology.

My imperturbable friend sat and smoked. Stopping before him again, I humbly asked his best judgment.

"Accept."

"That means fight."

A shrug.

"Doesn't acceptance insure a meeting?"

"No."

These monosyllables became exasperating. An idea occurred to me.

"Say," said I, "come to my room and we will have a small bottle together and talk this matter over."

That was a stroke of genius. A single glass loosened his reluctant tongue, and in five minutes I got more from him than could have been extracted by the dry process in five hours. In his experience, there were twenty or more challenges in Mexico to one meeting, fifty meetings to one fatality. Benavides reckoned on my declining and wanted the prestige of it. This would subject me to insult and probable outrage. A prompt acceptance, however, would force him to show his colors.

"And even if he fights, you can hold your own," he said.

"But I have no skill with sword or pistol," I protested. The only weapon I had used in years was the shotgun, with which I had a record of nineteen clay pigeons out of twenty, at thirty yards.

"Make it shotguns, then, thirty yards — crack a pigeon — kill a greaser."

I shuddered at the bare possibility. But another bottle decided me.

"I'll teach the coward never to dare an American," said I. To my shame be it told, at the dictation of the Stubby Man, I wrote the usual letter of acceptance, handing it to him for delivery to General Alatorre.

"You're a brick, old boy," he said quite jovially, and went on his damnable mission. A minute afterward, I regretted what I had done. The folly of it seemed suddenly plain. I started after him. Which way had he gone? I inquired and followed. I saw him about a block distant and ran as rapidly as I could. Coming within a hundred feet, I hallooed, for I was nearly out of breath, and he was going fast. "Say! Hi there! Whoop! — " a hand stopped me short. Two policemen stood there with drawn clubs, and the one who held me had his head bandaged. I tried to

H

explain, but excitement and breathlessness lost me what little Spanish I knew. In spite of protest and even proffer of money, I was hustled along to the jail. I had hopes for an instant, when I mentioned money, for one of the fellows paused and muttered something to the other whose head was bandaged, but the latter retorted negatively and fiercely, and on we went. At the jail, the Fat Official entered my name and a charge of disorderly conduct. I presented my card and offered security. But to no purpose. I threatened to appeal to the American consul. At the name, the Fat Official laughed. " El Consul Leech ! " he said contemptuously. " El Consul verde ! " He had evidently no respect for Leech. By mere chance, I had with me my passport. It was a formidable document with big seal and much red tape. Drawing it from my pocket and opening it slowly so that all its importance was displayed, I held it up and demanded that the consul be sent for. The Fat Official was evidently impressed. Perceiving this, I assumed a loftier dignity and proclaimed my determination to have heavy damages and satisfaction for the outrage. " Soy un ciudadano Americano, y estoy bajo la proteccion del Presidente de los Estados Unidos. Tenga Vd. cuidado ! " said I, pointing to one policeman — he shrank back —

"y Vd. tambien," pointing to the other who wilted — "y Usted, Señor," pointing to the Fat Official, and he grew visibly nervous. At each phrase, I brandished the sealed and ribboned passport. The Fat Official tried to explain. I waved him off. " Esperaré aqui hasta que venga el Consul Americano," said I, imperiously.

"Sirvase Vd.," said the Fat Official, humbly, "sirvase Vd. esperar en este cuarto." He opened the door of an adjoining room, and asked me to enter, bowing as if I were a prince. I entered, and there, sitting complacently, was Jesus Delaney.

CHAPTER XV

JESUS looked up, sprang forward, and before I could stop him threw his arms round my neck and kissed me on both cheeks. Now, I don't like demonstrative greetings or leave-takings of any sort, but this special form is offensively foreign, distinctly and intolerably un-American. Once on an election day at home, I saw two drunken ticket peddlers thus seal their maudlin admiration, and it almost turned my stomach. Jesus seemed to realize I didn't like it. "Pardon me, sir," he said; "I am so happy."

There was the outlandishness of it again — smashed on the sconce and kept three days in jail for nothing — yet, because he sees a man little more than a stranger to him, he becomes ecstatic. It flattered me, however, for it showed great affection in the fellow.

"Happy! In jail?" I remonstrated.

His face beamed, his eyes were glorious.

"Yes, to you it is a jail, to me it is a holy place, sanctified, celestial!"

Alas! In those restless eyes was the unmistakable gleam of madness.

"Calm yourself, my poor boy. Be calm. All will be well," I said soothingly.

"All is well. All is heaven for me," he murmured.

Clearly, he was daft. That terrible blow on the head had overthrown reason.

"Has Doctor Medina called to see you?" I asked anxiously.

"No doctor has seen me. Do I look as if I needed a doctor?" He drew himself up, a magnificent model of physical health and strength. The thick, straight hair shut out any trace of a wound. But those eyes — how they glowed and burned!

"I am in heaven. In heaven," he repeated.

My God! What a pity, thought I, such a mind in such a frame, blighted perhaps forever. Oh! the villains who had brought him to this! I sought to quiet him.

"Be calm, my boy, come sit down by me. Tell me what has happened. I am your friend. Do not fear to tell me all. Be calm — be calm."
An expression of surprise crossed his face.

"I did not mean to tell anybody. But you are my friend, are you not? You are my friend!" He seized both my hands with a convulsive grasp, and as suddenly dropped them.

"Yes, surely, Jesus, I am your friend. Confide in me, poor boy."

"You will understand my happiness. I know you will."

Then, with that maniacal glare still in his eyes, which he kept fixed on mine, he thrust his right hand under his vest. I became uneasy. Had he a weapon concealed? "Be calm, my boy, be calm," I repeated, eying him closely and prepared for any emergency. Slowly, ecstatically, he drew forth, not a weapon, but a small, dainty-looking envelope.

He gazed at it a moment, then kissed it rapturously, while I became conscious of a faint, sweet perfume. Taking from the envelope a little note, he handed it to me.

"Read," he said in low, trembling tones.

I took the note and adjusted my spectacles. It was from Marie Romero, the Governor's daughter. With delicately worded sympathy she promised his speedy release, and expressed the tender hope that she would see him in person. That was all.

Yes, in truth Jesus was mad, mad with a lunacy

that comes betimes to every son of Adam, to every daughter of Eve, a lunacy that has its lights and shades, its storm and calm, its lucid intervals, — the lunacy of love.

Nature is a marvel in Mexico. It knows no bounds, follows no course. It is full of surprises and excesses. A cloudless day blackens at once to furious tempest. Prolonged, blistering, gasping heat gives instant place to chilling mist. To-day the plain lies parched and dead, to-morrow, glorious with grass and flowers. Thus material nature —is it so with man? I thought of Jesus as I first met him, gentle, pious, absorbed in his divine mission; then recalled that scene on the plaza where he stood defiant, disfigured, a savage. Now here he was again transformed, another being, rapturous, ecstatic, heart and soul aglow! And why this latest paroxysm? Just a scented note, nicely written, doubtless, and properly worded, but for all that of no consequence, nothing to excite any man in his senses. It had reached him shortly before my arrival, and he was for some reason at once transferred from the solitary cell in which he had been confined, to the comfortable quarters where I found him. The writer was the good angel who wrought the change.

I could not induce Jesus to relate his experience.

His present happiness blotted out all recollections of past unpleasantness. To him the affair on the plaza was the most fortunate incident of his life. "But for that," he asked, "what would my life have been worth?"

"Your life didn't seem worth much as it was." I answered dryly. "Have you seen the Reverend Lamb yet?"

"No, you are my first visitor."

"And I am an unwilling one, in fact a prisoner like yourself." I plumped this at him purposely, hoping the news might startle him out of his sentimental dreamland. It did. The love-light fled from his face and he stared at me.

"You a prisoner? What has happened?"

I began my story and he listened breathlessly. When I got as far as the Benavides' challenge and my acceptance he sprang to his feet.

"You shall not fight him. It would be wrong," he exclaimed.

"My own opinion exactly," said I, glad to see that he took such a sensible view of it.

I proceeded to relate how I had reconsidered and tried to recall my acceptance, but failed to catch the Stubby Man.

"I am glad you failed," he said.

"Glad I failed! What do you mean?"

" I mean that the fight is mine."

" Yours ! "

" Yes, mine.   He struck me down, the coward," — again there came that ugly curl of the lip and that savagery of teeth and eyes.   " He must give me satisfaction first."

" You forget," said I, remonstrating.   " You forget you are a minister."

" I am a Mexican," he answered, and his manner was magnificent.

" You are a missionary," I protested.

" I am a Mexican," he repeated, " and know what honor demands : I will fight him."

" But what will the Reverend Lamb think of you if you do ? "

" What would she think of me if I did not ? " and he held up the scented letter and kissed it.

He was soaring again, so I brought him back to solid ground.

" How would Miss Anderson regard such a thing ? "

At the name he started and thrust the letter back in his bosom with a pained expression.   He was silent.   I pressed my advantage.

" They are all anxious about you at the Institute. Poor Miss Anderson particularly.   Would it not be well to send her word ?   It will greatly relieve her."

He raised his eyes and there was an almost pitiable look in them.

"Are you sure," he asked slowly, " Miss Anderson cares very much?"

"Why, of course, I presumed from the relations between you,— "

" I do not ask your presumptions," he interrupted almost rudely. "You spoke of her particularly. Did she," and his big eyes held me fast, "show any particular feeling?"

"Well, not exactly feeling, but — "

"I knew it," he cried, "I knew it! she has none!"

Evidently Brother Lamb had not brought matters as far as he imagined.

"Some people don't show their feelings," I argued, "there can be great goodness — "

"The heart craves more than mere goodness!" he burst out. "I see it all now. There is piety that is passionless, religion that alienates nature, philanthropy that is sordid." I could not make clear the relevancy of this, but he was letting loose on a subject of which he was full, and for which I had little relish. So it was a relief to me when in the midst of his harangue there was heard the tread of heavy feet, the clang of arms, and the door suddenly opened to usher in his Excellency Governor

Romero. We arose. The Governor addressed
Jesus in Spanish, but in a tone and manner I knew
to be friendly and apologetic, then stretched forth
his hand, which Jesus shook warmly.

"Esta Usted en libertad, Señor," said the Governor to Jesus. "Venga Vd. conmigo." He
placed his arm within that of Jesus, but the latter
drew back and asked a question, pointing to me.
I understood him to be stating my case to his
Excellency. He spoke rapidly, energetically, and
ended by presenting me. The Governor shook
my hand quite cordially ; I presented him my card
and showed him my passport. He glanced at both.

"Vengan, Caballeros," he said. "Vengan am-
bos conmigo " (Come, gentlemen'! Come with me,
both of you !).

We followed him out. His eye fell sternly on
the Fat Official and he administered a fierce rebuke.
Then he called for the policemen who had arrested
me.

"Adonde estan esos policias?" he asked. The
Fat Official humbly brought them in. They quailed
before the great man, who scored them in most
merciless Spanish.

"Caballeros, mi coche esta a su disposicion."
He insisted on our entering his carriage, which he
ordered driven to my hotel, where Jesus and my-

self left him with mutual protestations of gratitude
and esteem.

Elated with the change in my fortune, I took
the arm of my young friend and brought him to
my room.   Jesus was very abstemious at the
Institute, a little claret was his only indulgence;
but on my insisting, he agreed to share with me
the contents of a delicious bottle of Pommery.
What a wholesome sound comes from drawing a
cork!   It is the overture to the opera of good fellowship the world over.   We clinked and drained
a glorious glass and gazed at each other in great
good humor.   What an escapade it had been and
how happily ended.   Here there was a rap at the
door, and without further ado in came my forgotten messenger of war, my prospective second
in a duel, the Stubby Man.   The whole devilish
difficulty came back to me.

"Well," I asked anxiously, "what have you
done?"

"All."

"Did you see General Alatorre?"

"Yes."

He was at his damned monosyllables again.   I
could not bear them.

"Sit down here, man, and drink—drink this."
I filled my own glass, which he emptied.   An-

other and then another, Jesus looking on in astonishment.

"Now then," said I, "tell your story."

He did, and with an easy fluency, even flippancy, that was remarkable. He had met the General and communicated my message. The General had taken exceptions to the weapons I named.

"Thank God!" I ejaculated.

"Referred to Article 12 of the Code."

"Good!" I exclaimed.

"Asked for time to consult his principal."

"Give him time," I said.

"He made some reflections," he continued, "on shotguns, which I took personally." Here the Stubby Man deliberately filled another glass.

"I asked for an apology then and there. Same was refused. Challenge issued, accepted, and duel fixed for the morning at six o'clock." He drank his glass with calm composure.

"A duel! You to fight a duel on such a trivial cause!"

"Fought 'em for triviALLer," he replied.

"And to-morrow morning. Good God, man! on the Sabbath! What do you mean?"

"You are to be my second," he answered, again filling his glass.

"Never! Never! I'm done with the whole barbarous business. I shall leave this lawless country."

"Do you hesitate to do for me what you asked me to do for you?" The Stubby Man spoke slowly and with dignity.

This put the matter in a new light. I was hesitating to answer, when up spoke Jesus:—

"Excuse me, Mr. —— "

"Craig," said the Stubby Man.

"Mr. Craig, my friend is an aged man. His life has made such a duty as you propose unsuitable and improper. But if you must have a second under the circumstances, I'll be your second."

"So be it," said Craig, promptly; "let us drink to the bargain."

I protested. "No! No! Young man. You say that such a duty is unsuitable and improper for me, how much more so for you; you forget what you are."

He reddened. "We argued that before tonight. No use going over the ground again. Mr. Craig, I will join you in the morning."

Overcome by my feelings I could only sit and listen to them as they talked over the cold-blooded details. Presently Craig arose, shook hands, and with the remark that a man whose life depends on a steady hand in the morning should keep a clear head at night, he took his departure.

No argument could change the resolution of Jesus. He made light of all I said and soon retired to the room adjoining mine, which I had secured for him. I went to bed, but could not sleep. I felt my own responsibility for the whole occurrence; my miserable weakness had brought it on; this young man's career would be blighted. The more I thought of the matter, the worse it looked. Strange that it did not occur to me to seek counsel with Lamb or Leech; but it didn't. Finally I sprang from my bed, determined to see Jesus again and strive to change him. I entered his room, for the door, as is common in Mexico, was open. He lay sound asleep. The tropical moon shone through the window, lighting up his face as with a glory. I will never forget the picture. He was the only human being I ever saw who was beautiful in sleep. I could not bring myself to wake him and stole softly away.

CHAPTER XVI

THE DUEL

ALL night I lay restless, and at the first break of day sought the room of Jesus. Entering quietly, as I did not know whether he was yet awake, I perceived him kneeling by his bedside and praying aloud. I caught the words: "O God! mark the ways of Thy servant and make them Thine! Guide his footsteps to Thy throne! Cause him to live as is meet in Thine eyes, whatsoever the murmurings of men." Then followed the Lord's Prayer, fervent and pathetic. I waited until "Forgive us our trespasses as we forgive those who trespass against us," when I placed my hands on his shoulders and said solemnly, "Young man, with those words on your lips, can you dare begin this day as you decided last night?" He rose as I was speaking; the devout expression on his face deepened momentarily, then gave way to one of gay good humor.

"Missed your vocation. Ought to have been a

preacher," was his laughing response, and ere I could rejoin, in came Craig with a small satchel in one hand and what seemed a long violin case in the other. He must have had a drink or two, for he was in high feather and talkative.

"Morning! No weapons named last night, so brought pops," holding up the little satchel, "and prickers," holding up the long case. Here were the instruments of death. I shuddered at the sight of them and was speechless.

"Just time get cup coffee," he continued, "and drive grounds. Doctor Bradley downstairs waiting. Let's go."

Off they started. In mute protest I followed.

In the hotel lobby, Doctor Bradley, a distinguished-looking man, joined us, and after a hasty cup of coffee we rode to the appointed place. Along the route all three laughed and joked, heedless of their mission or of me, and on alighting were indifferent to a sight that chilled my blood. Two men with pale faces were bearing from the field a corpse.

"Some early bird," remarked Craig.

"Whom the worms have caught," said the Doctor.

We walked a short distance and came in sight of a party of four, among whom I recognized the

I

General and Benavides. The latter started toward us.

"That tall man approaching is Benavides," said I to Jesus. He gave a quick glance and his face hardened.

"He's the second," said Craig. "Meet him. Make it pistols, any distance, or swords. Leave all him."

Jesus advanced until they met, and both bowed ceremoniously. There was a short conference, and Jesus returned.

"Pistols," he said, "twenty paces."

The ground was measured with deliberate care, and weapons examined. Every move of the dread drama was to me a horrible nightmare, but Jesus was as calm and collected as if duelling had been taught him at the Institute. I swear he seemed to enjoy it. At last the men were placed, the word given, and the shots rang out. I saw Craig clasp his hand to the side of his head, and I ran to him.

"Are you hurt?"

"No!" he answered. "T'other fellow." His opponent was down. A dark red mark told where the bullet singed along Craig's temple.

Benavides came forward.

"My principal is wounded," said he in English, addressing Jesus. "His honor is satisfied."

Jesus bowed.

"So the affair of our friends is concluded," said Benavides, smiling and extending his hand.

"The affair of our friends, yes," said Jesus; "but have not you and I a little matter to adjust?"

Benavides looked astonished. "I have never met you before, sir," he answered.

"Not to my face," said Jesus, his eyes ablaze; "but you came behind my back on last Wednesday night at the plaza, like a coward, and struck me down. Blow for blow!" It was only the open palm, but so lustily Benavides almost fell.

Here was another horror.

We saw Benavides consulting with his friends. Then one of the latter advanced.

"Act for me," said Jesus to Craig.

"Turn about," said Craig, and went to meet the emissary. In a few seconds he returned.

"Challenged fight immediately," said he. "Name weapons."

"Say to his second that if his principal agrees to a peaceful settlement of the affair with my friend here without apology, I will give him the choice of weapons."

This was said to Craig in a low tone and in Spanish, so that I did not know the purport till afterward. The seconds consulted again, and shortly Craig announced the conditions accepted and swords the weapons.

Whistling a lively air he opened the long case. There were three swords in it. "Look, Jesus! Butes!" he said.

Picking up each in turn, Jesus scanned it closely and in a moment announced his choice. I saw Benavides, his coat and vest removed and his right arm bare to the elbow, whirling his sword and flashing it right and left. He was evidently an expert. A great fear came on me.

"Jesus," I cried, "you must not fight! Craig, this is murder. The boy knows —"

"His own business," interrupted Craig. "Look!" He pointed to Jesus, who had also bared his arm and was making his weapon writhe and dart and hiss like a fiery serpent.

"My aged friend, you are in Mexico. Don't forget it."

As if I were likely to forget it!

At a signal the contestants advanced, saluted, lowered their weapons and stood in position.

A quick question, a joint response, and steel met steel. Both were masters. Both were matched. Benavides had the advantage in practice, Jesus in strength. Benavides was fighting to kill. There was malice, hate, murder, in every stroke. Jesus was fighting for God knows what, maybe revenge, maybe for my sake, maybe there were thoughts of a señorita whose little scented letter lay on his heart; but whatever nerved him, he was calm, swift, confident. His handsome face, glowing eyes, and graceful, chivalrous bearing were sublime. Now there is an animal in every man that loves a fight; in me it is an animal of fairly good development, and it soon was roused. Every stroke gave me a thrill. Once such terrible joy upbounded in my soul when Jesus seemed gaining a slight advantage that I could no longer hold myself, and I shouted at the top of my voice, "Give it to him, Jesus! Pink him!"

There was a deep murmur among the Mexicans, and Craig and the Doctor both rebuked me. I had to watch the fight in silence, every nerve strained to an awful tension. It was give and take with honors even. At last Benavides played a low, unmanly trick. Feigning exhaustion, he retreated slowly, step by step, until he seemed almost to yield, when suddenly he leaped to one side and Jesus, taken by surprise, was stabbed deeply in the sword arm. I saw the red blood spurt. The seconds sprang forward and separated the combatants.

Tears came into my eyes; I could have blubbered like a baby.

"You are wounded, my poor boy." He was pale.

"Only a scratch," he said. "Bind it with my handkerchief. Quick!" Doctor Bradley sought to make an examination, but he repulsed him.

Here Craig approached. "Other side satisfied if you are. Let's call it off."

"Not yet," said Jesus, and there and then his face took on that fierce, ugly look, just as it did when on the plaza I told him to yield.

"But, man, you can't use that arm."

"I have two arms," he said, grasping his sword with his left hand.

"Well, you're boss," said Craig, and returned.

I beseeched Jesus to quit; as well have pleaded with a panther. He was no more the missionary, mild and amiable; the glittering eyes, the teeth gleaming below the upcurled lip, the deadly, demoniac look proclaimed the savage.

Once more the men were placed and the word given.

Benavides now seemed to have the battle to himself. He was clearly on the offensive, and several vicious lunges he made, almost reached their aim. Fierce with the black hate of a bad heart, he had already an air of a merciless triumph. It remained but to finish his foe. Yet every effort failed. Jesus had a left nearly as good as his right, and its swordsmanship was more deceptive. After a succession of desperate strokes and stabs, the sword of Benavides flew from his grasp. Let me here admit that for a coward Benavides showed great courage. Folding his arms he looked Jesus full defiance. And Jesus, — I hate to write it, — but I could not help seeing the triumph in his face take on a sudden, sheer ferocity. He glared without pity at his weaponless foe, and raised his arm for the death stroke.

"My God, man, don't!" I cried. But I would have spoken in vain had not Craig with a swift leap stayed the uplifted arm.

CHAPTER XVII

WE BREAKFAST

"A FEW years ago," said Doctor Bradley, as he proceeded to wash and dress the wounded arm, "a cut like this would have been troublesome, now with antiseptic treatment there is little or no danger.   It will heal within a few days."

"There," said Craig to me in an undertone, "is one who formerly ranked at the head of his profession in Philadelphia."

"Travelling in Mexico?"

"No; settled."

"Why did he leave Philadelphia?"

"Skipped."

I inquired no further.   Many an American's residence in Mexico is shadowed with that suggestive word.   Some woman or some trust betrayed, menace of exposure, dread of punishment, the wretch takes refuge in exile.

We breakfasted together, for it was yet early in the day when we reached the hotel.   I had been informed of the condition of the last duel, and how

it relieved me of any concern for myself. I confess it helped my appetite. Not that I was afraid;
I fear no man — not I. It was inborn principle
that revolted against this monstrous method of
settling difficulties between man and man.

It was pleasing to me and edifying, too, in view
of the events of the day, to see that Jesus, when
the meal was set before us, did not forget his pious
teachings. The Doctor was chatting freely as he
adjusted his napkin, Craig had already seized knife
and fork, and I myself was about to begin, when my
eye was caught by a pleading look from the lad.
It was a comprehensive look, for it affected the
Doctor and even Craig as it did me, and without
a word we bowed our heads. Jesus said grace.

" You're not hardened to Mexican dishes yet, I
see," said Doctor Bradley to me. I was turning
over curiously a greenish compound of some sort.

"Don't be afraid; it's better than it looks."

"It's delicious," said Jesus, taking a huge
mouthful.

"Good!" urged Craig, and thus encouraged I
took a little of the stuff on my fork and dubiously
tried it. For a full minute my mouth was a fur-
nace. What would have happened had I not
spat the fiery morsel on my plate? The others
laughed.

"You will like it in time," said the Doctor.

"Never!" I gasped. (But as a matter of fact I have grown since to a real fondness for chili verde.)

Before the meal was finished the waiter handed me an elaborate envelope, which I found to contain a formal invitation to a dinner from Governor Romero. I handed it to Jesus, by whom it was more fully translated.

"I am sorry he didn't include you in the invitation," said I.

"A poor teacher in a Mission School is not a suitable guest for a governor," he replied, with a bitterness in the voice very unusual.

"Speaking of the Mission School, I think it may be as well to keep from the Reverend Lamb all knowledge of to-day's episode."

"Oh! he'll hear of it; some one will be sure to tell him."

"Then I had best be the one," said I, "and the sooner the better."

So I accompanied Jesus to the Institute.

On the way we met Consul Leech, who greeted us effusively.

"Didn't I bring the Governor to time?" he exclaimed, grinning. "And two birds with one stone, as it were?" and he forced an unpleasant laugh.

"When did you see the Governor?" I asked.

"I did not see him," he grinned. "Immediately on receipt of your message last night, announcing your arrest, I drove to his house. He was not in. But I left him a strong appeal for you and our friend Jesus. I did not expect such prompt compliance; but I tell you I made it strong," he grinned. "I made it very strong, and I got there all right! I got there!" He chuckled as if thoroughly convinced that he was a downright good fellow as well as a model consul. I had great doubts even then whether his appeal, strong as it was, had played any part whatever in our release, nor was I surprised when subsequently informed by the Governor himself that the Consul's appeal was merely a letter asking for an interview, and that the letter did not reach him until the day after our release.

Nevertheless a leading New York paper (of which Leech was a frequent correspondent) came out a week or so later with big head-lines:—

Plucky Consul Leech! Beards the Mexican Lion in his Den! Demands the Release of an American Citizen imprisoned at Alameda. Pleads for an Imprisoned Protestant Minister! Liberates Both!!!

Then followed a much-distorted and sensational account, in which Jesus and myself were the merest satellites of the consular luminary Leech.

Oh dear! of what shoddy stuff reputations are made! If I were Secretary of State for one hour, I would twist the useless necks of nine-tenths of these Leeches — but why talk!

CHAPTER XVIII

Jesus was cordially welcomed at the Institute. Reverend Lamb expressed his thanksgiving in prayer. Nos. 1, 2, and 3 snivelled and snickered by turns. Miss Anderson extended her hand, shrivelled and tentacular, and hoped his experience would be a lesson to him.

"And to you," she added, looking hard at me.

"Were you severely wounded?" she asked.

"No; only a mere scratch on the arm."

"On the arm! He told me on the head!" and she turned on me once more.

I was saved from explanation by the entrance of Mrs. Lamb, who embraced Jesus with genuine affection. Had he been her son she could not have shown more joy or pride. All was congratulation and rejoicing, even among the servants. I observed Antonio run in rubbing his hands and shaking his head, look at Jesus, and laughing gleefully dart out, then in a few seconds reappear to go through the same pantomime. He seemed beside himself, and I was wondering how he could be calmed, when a vagrant cat which was the object of his vigilant animosity, because it preyed on his feathered pets, happened to appear in the patio; he became absorbed in the relentless chase that ensued.

As soon as I could take the Reverend Lamb aside I told the story of the duel, putting as favorable a phase on it as possible. He was not shocked nor seemingly sorry. On the contrary, just as had happened when I told him of the arrest, he appeared involuntarily to beam with satisfaction. Again he must have observed my surprise; for there was a quick twitching of the facial muscles, settling at last into clerical solemnity.

"Ah, an unfortunate affair! An unfortunate affair!" he ejaculated.

"But unavoidable," I urged.

"I fear its effect on our work. Benavides is a power in Alameda."

"But Benavides is satisfied. He ought to be. He came out without a scratch."

"Yes, by the magnanimity of Jesus — that very fact will be galling to his pride." I hadn't told the Reverend Lamb how little of magnanimity

his pupil had displayed.   It could do no good.
But I assured him that the trouble was over.

"Well, we will see, we will see ; we must make
the best of it."

Here the Reverend Lamb was interrupted by
the entry of Jesus, who with joyful gesture held
up for our inspection a letter.   It was an invitation he had just received to dine with Governor
Romero.

It came most seasonably, bringing happiness to
the heart of Jesus and relieving the misgivings of
the Reverend Lamb.   For favor with the Governor meant peace with his son-in-law.

"Come, Jesus, come both of you; let us to
prayer meeting.   We have special cause this day
to give praise to Him 'from whom all blessings
flow.'"

It was the Sunday morning meeting.   In the
little church the teachers were all gathered, Miss
Anderson at the organ with the larger pupils, and
some fifteen or twenty whom the Reverend Lamb
informed me were converts from Rome.   Near
the door sat a woman in deep mourning, who
when Jesus entered fell on her knees and bowed
her head, sobbing.   It was his mother.   But he
did not see her.

With the exception of a few respectable old

ladies who sat apart with Mrs. Lamb, most of
the converts impressed me unfavorably.   There
were stupid faces among them, and some I
would not care to meet on a lonesome road;
but you can't judge by appearances.   I know a
most exemplary member of my own congregation
who always reminds me of Captain Kidd.   Besides, if these converts were as bad as they
looked, all the more remarkable their conversion.

There was a long Spanish prayer by the Reverend Lamb and a hymn in Spanish.   Then followed
a prayer by Jesus, which seemed to reach the
hearts of all by its intensity.   Could this be the
same face I had seen but a few hours before,
cruel, devilish — incarnate ferocity ?   The sweetness, the lovableness, the trustful innocent charm
of it!   And the voice round, full, resonant, a
tender, touching music in every tone, and the
eyes alight with faith and the simple candor of
a child!   Could it be the same ?   At the close
of the prayer by Jesus there was another hymn,
and then a well-dressed man in front whom I
had noticed among the converts, but whose face
I did not see, arose to pray.   I recognized Doctor Medina.   He prayed in English.   I had had
doubts of him from his failure to see Jesus or
report to me at the hotel, but his present ap-

pearance and the prayer removed them. He was the personification of piety. Those deep-brown, honest, soulful eyes uplifted, lips quivering and voice vibrating with pathos, he beseeched God to deliver his countrymen from the errors of Rome. He thanked Him for the Institute and the great good wrought by its teachers. He thanked Him particularly for the Reverend Lamb. Then he referred to Jesus and his recent trial. Tenderly, delicately, ever more feelingly until his heart overflowed and tears rolled down his cheeks. Teachers, pupils, converts, were overcome, while Jesus himself sobbed aloud. It was the climax of the meeting. I doubt if many heard the sweetly sung hymn that brought the services to a close.

" That prayer of Doctor Medina was the most affecting I ever listened to," said I to Jesus, as we were passing out.

" Doctor Medina? Whom do you mean ? " he answered in a surprised tone.

"Why, is not that Doctor Medina ? " I inquired, pointing to him.

" Doctor Medina! No! That's Brother Baez, one of the Reverend Lamb's recent converts. He was once a priest, but recanted Romanism and became — "

K

"A confidence man," I blurted out excitedly, and told my experience. "Here is his card." The fellow evidently remembered me, for before I could get to him he slunk out of the room.

Jesus looked mortified. "You must tell this to the Reverend Lamb. He ought to be exposed."

I told the Reverend Lamb. He raised his eyes and displayed the first genuine feeling I had noticed in him, as he muttered, half to himself, —

"Heavenly Father, is there an honest man among them?"

CHAPTER XIX

Desirous of making a good impression on the occasion of the Governor's dinner, I made careful inquiry regarding such affairs and informed myself fully on every detail of dress and etiquette. I also applied with much zeal to that portion of "Spanish at a Gulp" which covered conversation at table. I found it hard work, yet managed to acquire an easy mastery of quite a number of necessary phrases and sentences, such as: "Mucho me alegro de ver a Usted, Sirvase Usted pasar el pan, Puedo ofrecer a Usted la mantequilla? Permite que le llene el vaso."

I tried one or two of these with questionable success on the hotel waiter. He was, however, a stupid fellow and probably hard of hearing, for I had to repeat and re-repeat, so that the fine effect was destroyed. But the proprietor of the hotel, whose aid I also sought, assured me most solemnly that my pronunciation was perfect and that I would readily pass for a Castilian.

So I had every confidence of carrying myself becomingly. I was worried, however, about Jesus. The Institute afforded sad training for such functions, and I feared that his social experience at college was little better. True, he had that gracious gentleness, the soul of courtesy, which seems to follow the slightest strain of Spanish blood, and he was a graceful, well-built, handsome fellow. Even these advantages, however, require certain touches and trimmings which are not born with a man and can only be acquired by experience. I remember how long it took me at the Naval Academy to wear off the crude edges and awkward ways of the country. It was near the close of my last term before I felt at ease.

Poor Jesus was not what you would call clerical looking, but he usually wore a sort of uniform procured by Reverend Lamb which was sombre and dull. If he had no better, and of course he hadn't, it would really be embarrassing.

Such were my thoughts of him as I started leisurely to dress for the dinner. Good clothes are the complement of the gentleman. Nobody despises foppery more than I; but nobody takes a more honest satisfaction in being well dressed, and, if I must say it, advancing years have only rounded my figure to that comfortable fulness which so well becomes a dress suit.

Properly and elaborately apparelled after much effort, I was contemplating myself in the mirror and reflecting how much it was to be regretted that I had not another such outfit for Jesus, when a soft tap at the door announced him. He entered. Alas! he was in his everyday Institute costume! If anything, it seemed duller and shabbier than usual. It was too bad. But of course I made no comment. It wasn't the poor lad's fault.

"Dressed already, I see," he said, evidently struck with my appearance.

"Yes; just a few duds," said I, almost apologetically.

"There is plenty of time, is there not?"

"Oh! ample time."

"Passe! Passe! Señor!" he called aloud, and to my surprise a mozo entered carrying two huge bundles.

"These are mine," said Jesus. "May I take the liberty of using your room?"

"Oh! certainly, certainly! But what have you there?"

"Just a few duds," said he, laughing, and open-

ing a bundle, he held up for my inspection, of all
things, a new dress suit.

The other bundle disclosed hat box with silk hat,
patent leather pumps, stockings, collars, cuffs, ties,
studs, as complete an assortment as I had myself.

"It comes high," said Jesus, "but I had to have
it.   May I dress here?"

"Certainly," and at the word he flung off his
clerical-looking clothes and stood before me without a stitch on him.

Travellers in lands inhabited by dark-skinned
people have told us how different from ours are
their ideas of decency.   Exposure, which at home
would shock the most brazen, is there looked on as
a matter of course.   Climate, you say? Not at all.
Japan is in the north temperate zone, yet there the
sexes mingle indiscriminately in the public baths.

Has not color something to do with it?   Light-
haired playmates of mine in boyhood always seemed
more sensitive than dark haired, the brunette bolder
than the blonde.

May not nature, when she shades the human skin,
at the same time dim the sense of delicacy?   No
American youth, however coarse or calloused, would
have done as Jesus did.   Yet none in my belief
was freer from any taint of personal impurity —
his the unconscious innocence of a child of nature.

" How good it feels to strip," he said, inflating his chest and throwing back his shoulders. Alas! I lost my complacent pride in my own attire.

What tailor's art could add to that magnificent physique? Every garment would but hide its glory. I felt old, fat, misshapen, before this perfect man.

And how easily he dressed! The silk stockings slipped over his bare feet, the snowy linen sought the broad breast, neck and wrists received their due adornment, one garment followed another until in a jiffy it was done. Before my eyes the minister had wrought a double transformation. First a god in bronze, then a well-groomed society man! I did not ask any questions — I was too astonished. It would have seemed to me in keeping with the rest if the mozo who brought in the bundles, like some fabled fairy godmother, had with a wave of his sombrero called forth a coach and six.

THE DINNER PARTY

THE Governor received us with that refined blending of dignity and deference which is the birthright of every Mexican, and introduced his wife, who seemed (as do so many Mexican women) much older than her husband. Again my language faculty failed.. Phrases culled with such care from "Spanish at a Gulp" withered and died. Sentences I thought to be under thorough discipline became a wordy rabble. I labored away, using just Spanish enough to make my English unintelligible. But the host and hostess with perfect good breeding pretended to understand me when I did not understand myself, and put me so entirely at ease, it gave me courage to continue. Presently the daughter entered, graciously shook hands with me and even more cordially, it seemed, with Jesus. Now even an American youth under the circumstances might feel embarrassed and blush and blunder. But Jesus turned white and trembled. I feared he was about to faint. (That is the one thing I detest in him — he's over-emotional.) I helped him out with a flashing reminiscence of "Spanish at a Gulp": "Me alegro mucho, yes indeed ah! of course it is, de ver a Usted — muy mucho, Señorita."

"Si," her laugh was the sweetest little laugh; lips, teeth, eyes, all made merry music. Nobody could resist it. Even Jesus rallied.

"Señorita," he murmured, "debo dar las gracias a Usted por —" but here his voice faltered and his eyes filled. Turning quickly away, I addressed the old couple an inquiry which required their whole attention and violent facial contortions and manual gestures of mine to make sense of, but I had the satisfaction of seeing the young couple clasp hands and look happy.

Other guests now appeared and the gorgeously furnished parlors became enlivened. I got along famously by bowing and smiling indiscriminately, and I saw that Jesus maintained his vantage ground with the señorita. Indeed, I began to worry lest she was neglecting other duties, when suddenly she darted from him and ran with outstretched hands to welcome some one specially favored. It was Benavides.

All seemed to be awaiting him, for immediately

on his entry the guests were paired and marched to the dining room. I had the distinguished honor of escorting the Governor's wife, while the hapless Jesus led in an old dowager, whose face, despite its wrinkles, was elaborately painted and calcimined. Seated opposite him were Miss Romero and Señor Benavides. I did not observe the latter until near the close of the meal, by which time, the sumptuous viands and the rich wines which, let me say, my hostess compelled me out of sheer gallantry to partake beyond my usual limit, made me well disposed to all mankind. So when I did notice him, such was my genial humor, I do believe, had I caught the scoundrel's eye, I would have raised my glass, as I was doing to all around, and drank his health.

It was a moment of great pride to me when the Governor rose in his seat and in words of elegant courtesy proposed my health. Now I have some repute at home as an after-dinner speaker, and my experience stood me in good stead. Arising, I bowed my best Naval Academy bow to the Governor, then another of the same sort to his wife, and a third encompassed the whole company. I spoke as follows: "No hablo good — I mean bueno Espagnol. Estoy Americano y hablo nothing — I mean todos los dias English — that is

Ingles.   Pero, nevertheless, quiero to say that
I appreciate — aprecio mucho esta courtesia y pro-
poso to drink, I mean beber la buen salud de la
Señora Romero."   The applause was hearty.

Cigars were lit, several of the ladies lighting
cigarettes, and after another toast or two all
strolled out into the magnificent inner-court
garden or patio.   The orchestra played a grand
march.   The scene recalled the Arabian Nights.

Soon the music softened, softened and seemed
to steal languorously into a dreamy Mexican waltz,
wiling the senses away with it.   Opening into the
patio was a great hall whose colored pillars and
rich mosaics were palatial.   Into this hall the host
led with his partner, I followed with Mrs. Romero,
and presently every guest was circling gayly
to the inspiring strains.   Every guest, did I say?
No, one pair sat apart.   Jesus couldn't dance.

What he must have suffered, seeing me and
thinking of the delight he was denying his partner by not having learned my accomplishments!
Nor could it have consoled him to witness Señorita
Romero gliding amorously round and round in
the arms of Señor Benavides.   The fourth time
I passed I noticed such downright agony in his
face that I thought to go to him.   Just then I
saw Benavides seat his partner.   An idea struck

me — one of those inspirations which we are wont to call presence of mind. Instead of going to Jesus I brought up near Benavides, seated Mrs. Romero beside him, and begged the honor of a dance from her daughter. She assented and away we went. On the very first round when we reached Jesus (I mention this to show my affection for the young man and the sacrifice of which I was capable), I stopped short and seated Miss Romero at his side, then craving a waltz from the old lady who was with him, off I sailed again. She was a poor waltzer and I was very tired, but I kept on. I was waltzing against time for friendship's sake. Whenever I passed the now happy Jesus I imagined I saw an imploring look flash from his dark eyes, bidding me go on, and on I went. Round and round I whirled until my head grew dizzy and I was at last forced to quit. Yet even then, as panting I approached Jesus, there was on his face such unmistakable protest that pleading the need of fresh air I paraded my aged partner in the patio.

*   *   *   *   *

Jesus was silent most of the way home and I was sleepy. I remember, however, that he roused me by a question, —

"Will you teach me how to waltz?"

I thought at first he was joking. But he wasn't.

CHAPTER XXI

JESUS A BEAR

THE morning after a late dinner and gay dance is apt to be given to moralizing. Thus it was that I lay in bed reflecting on recent occurrences in the life of Jesus Delaney and my personal responsibility in the premises. I acquitted myself of any design to bring about these events — nothing had been further from my thoughts. Yet unconsciously I had aided and abetted. I had met the young man little more than a week before, satisfied with his lot, engrossed in his sacred work, attached to a worthy woman, and following the lines laid down for him by his benefactors. Could this be said of him now? Certainly not. His mind was no longer on his work, his ambition was distorted, his relations with Miss Anderson strained if not broken, and above all and under all a foolish, hopeless passion for a girl in a different sphere of life.

Events had crowded. One by one they rose in my mind. The love-song at the market, the sight of Miss Romero on the plaza, the fight, the arrest, the release, the double duel, and last the dinner and dance. Where would such a pace lead? To no good in all human likelihood. I determined to consult with the Reverend Lamb, undo if I could the evil already done, and prevent if possible further mischief.

My opportunity for such counsel came that very day, as the Reverend Lamb, who, it seems, had been seized with misgivings himself, was an early caller at my room.

"I am here to speak with you about Jesus."

I knew what was coming and made no answer.

"He is acting very queerly of late, neglects his work, and" — the Reverend Lamb paused in the indictment — "he is almost rude to Miss Anderson."

"Impossible! He could not help being courteous."

"There are cases where mere courtesy is almost rudeness."

"Well, Jesus has had a very trying experience."

"I am aware of that."

"And I think a little time will bring him round."

"I trust so. But something happened yesterday I cannot account for by any reference to his experience."

The Reverend Lamb's solemn earnestness in making this statement was alarming. I could only dread some awful escapade compared with which the other affairs were trivial.

"Yesterday he drew his whole salary, instead of leaving it with me as usual, and he borrowed one hundred dollars additional." I was greatly relieved.

The dress suit was no more a mystery. I thought it best to tell all to the Reverend Lamb. I expected it would greatly amuse him. But instead he was amazed, incensed, roused into angry, bitter protest. Again did I marvel at his manner when informed of the arrest and the duel. These were serious, the dress suit a mere boyish vanity.

"It is wrong, all wrong, utterly demoralizing!" and he wrung his hands. I pleaded the natural desire of a young man to appear at his best on such an occasion.

"He was masquerading!" said the Reverend Lamb. "A minister of the Gospel in such a costume at a bacchanalian ball!"

"Reverend Lamb," said I, "there was nothing bacchanalian about the ball, nothing masquerading about the costume; I was there and similarly dressed."

"You are not a minister," he retorted.

"Thank God!" I answered.

"Amen!" said he, walking away. He had the last word. But he soon returned.

"You surely admit that, situated as he is, such conduct is folly," continued the Reverend Lamb.

There he had me. I could not deny the unseemliness of it from that standpoint.

"It is certainly to be regretted. I am deeply sorry to have been the occasion of it."

"What had best be done?" The Reverend Lamb was really anxious.

"Can you not send him off somewhere for a while?" I suggested.

He reflected. "I have it. The very thing. They want a missionary at Santa Rosa. A month there will remedy the whole trouble. But I must see Mrs. Lamb about it," and he left.

Sitting with Craig on the plaza that night watching the promenaders and listening to the music, I was surprised to see Jesus in the crowd, smartly dressed and walking by himself. He did not see us, but went round and round disconsolate. At last, after stopping and hesitating as if in doubt, he walked dejectedly away. We remained until the music ceased, and the night was so glorious we took a route to the hotel which led us by the house of Governor Romero. I paused to point it out to Craig, and as I did so, observed a tall, lonely figure in the shadow.

"Jesus," said Craig, "a bear." [1]

It was in truth Jesus.

We would have passed on, but his odd, fantastic actions held us. Even as we looked he removed his hat, stood on tiptoe and craned his neck, while his eyes were fixed in eager, ardent gaze upon an upper window. For a moment the curtain raised a tiny space, disclosing the fair hand that held it.

But during that moment the young man managed to fling more kisses and heave more sighs and writhe more visible ecstasy than has ever been told of in the maddest poetry of love. When the curtain fell he knelt. We walked away.

"What do you think of that?" I asked Craig.

He did not answer for some time, then I heard him growl under his breath, —

"Envy damned fool."

[1] When the young Mexican, in the course of his suit, reaches the point that brings him nightly to stand before the house of his lady-love, he is called "un oso," a bear.

L

CHAPTER XXII

A SPIRITUAL AWAKENING

THERE was a conference at the Institute on the following day between the Reverend and Mrs. Lamb and myself upon the subject of sending Jesus to Santa Rosa. The Reverend Lamb was strongly in favor of his being sent there, Mrs. Lamb was as strongly opposed. The Reverend Lamb deplored the gravity of the recent escapades, Mrs. Lamb made light of them. And when the Reverend Lamb rejoined by characterizing the whole conduct of Jesus as scandalous, Mrs. Lamb rose to his defence with spirit.

"What has the boy done," she asked, "that's so blamable? He saved the Governor's life. Was that scandalous? He defended himself against brutal policemen. What brave man would have done otherwise? Even the duel was more an impulse of friendship than the prompting of revenge. Did he not fight more on your account than his own?" she asked me. "If he went to a dinner party and dressed as other young men, or if he danced " (here Reverend Lamb raised his hands), "what harm?

" Jesus is no dowdy," she continued ; "and, even if true, for one of his years to be in love with a pretty girl — "

The entrance of Miss Anderson left the sentence unfinished, much to my regret ; for she had just reached a point upon which her candid opinion would have been of great interest.

The interruption caused some slight embarrassment, but it was readily relieved by the Reverend Lamb, who, to my astonishment, instead of changing the subject, plainly stated the question to Miss Anderson and virtually submitted it to her adjudication.

" We were discussing," said he, " the advisability of having Jesus for a time go to Santa Rosa in order that he may recover from the effects of his late unfortunate experiences."

" Not unfortunate — disgraceful is the proper word," and she eyed me sternly.

" Miss Anderson — " began Mrs. Lamb.

" My dear," interrupted her husband hastily, " I perceive some children in the flower-beds." There was a quick touch of color on the cheeks of Mrs. Lamb, but she quietly left the room.

"Disgraceful, not unfortunate," calmly repeated Miss Anderson.

The Reverend Lamb bowed his acquiescence.

"But do you not think that change of scene will remedy the evil?"

"Change of scene! Where in the Bible, Reverend Lamb, do you find change of scene prescribed for sin?"

The Reverend Lamb humbly acknowledged his error.

"What is needed is prayer," she said, "the constant society of the prayerful to lift one's mind from unholy thoughts. All that has happened is the doing of Satan. (Here she looked hard at me.) Let Satan be met here in Alameda, where Jesus has friends to help him, not in some far-away wilderness where he would have to cope with the enemy alone."

"You are right," said the Reverend Lamb, approvingly. "Let us pray."

Thus it came to pass there was a spiritual revival at the Institute. Prayers were longer, grace more impressive, meetings more frequent, and the battle against Rome waged with unwonted vigor. Jesus was unconscious of the cause or purpose of the unusual zeal. But he yielded to it. His emotional nature caught the heavenly fire, and soon he led all the rest in pious fervor. He was saved. Nay, more; the reaction from his worldly lapse carried him to a higher plane. In the schoolroom, in the church, but more marked in mission work, he became an evangelical giant. All he did was characterized by ardent, tireless, passionate energy. Everything alien to his holy purpose seemed forgotten. No more was he seen on the plaza, nor in lonely vigil at the residence of Miss Romero. Night and day his work went on. He prayed, sang, and preached. He made a house-to-house canvass in the poorest districts. Converts flocked to the Institute.

Every time I met the Reverend Lamb he had a tale of further conquest. Two more yesterday! Three to-day! No Indian could have been more boastful of scalps. Many who had backslidden returned to the fold. Doctor Medina (Brother Baez), among others, made open acknowledgment of his fall from grace. Deeply resentful of the fellow's fraud upon me, I expressed doubts to the Reverend Lamb of the genuineness of his repentance, but when he came to me one day at the Institute and, kneeling down in an attitude of profound shame and contrition, raised his tearful, pleading eyes and begged my pardon, I freely forgave him. Moreover, after I had lifted him to a seat beside me and heard from his lips the story of his life, the persecutions to which he was being subjected by relentless Rome, and the difficulties surrounding him by reason of his poverty, I was moved to help him with a donation.

Even Antonio gave promise of redemption, passing one whole Sunday without getting drunk. But Mrs. Lamb disappointed me. She who was so fit to lead, held aloof. I rarely saw her at a meeting. And stranger still, neither the Reverend Lamb nor any of the rest seemed to regret or even note her absence. She simply went her usual way, such time as she could spare being passed among the poor. While others prayed and preached to crowded gatherings, she sought the suffering in their wretched homes, remote from public gaze, dispensing charity, braving pestilence, nursing, consoling, encouraging.

Noble enough, no doubt; but, as the Reverend Lamb most justly asked, "of what avail to vanquish antichrist?"

No wonder she was unmentioned in his Report to the Board — a Report that will remain on record for all time, bearing testimony to the pious zeal, yea, and the business forethought of him who sent it.

"The spirit of the Gospel has at last descended

on Alameda," he wrote. "The cry of the benighted went forth; the answer has been heard
loud and clear, 'The Redeemer hath come.' We
have girded up our loins for a grand charge upon
the scarlet woman. To God be the glory given,
but let not be forgotten the meed of praise due to
the noble efforts of our brother in Christ, Jesus
Delaney. We need more money." And the next
draft remitted by the Board was a big one.

CHAPTER XXIII

A DISTURBED SERVICE

One of the new converts was the keeper of a cantina, who was known among the people as " El Pajaro," although his right name was Don Pancho Servando Realitos. (By the way, every Mexican has a nickname.) While El Pajaro's reform did not reach the extreme of closing his grog-shop, it went to the extent of renouncing Romanism and cock-fighting, to both of which evils he was formerly addicted. He was punctual at services and gave substantial evidence of sincerity by asking Jesus to visit his place and spread the true faith among its frequenters. So it was arranged that on a Sunday afternoon a Gospel gathering would be held at the cantina of El Pajaro. Thither I accompanied Jesus.

The little room was filled with men and women, and the bar where the unconverted wife of El Pajaro was discharging the functions of her converted husband, dealing out mescal, pulque, and cheap cigars to her customers, was enjoying an unusually brisk patronage. Several hulking loungers hung around the entrance, and in the back yard quite a crowd had gathered. Our arrival provoked no rowdyism. The scenes that are so common on such occasions at home — hooting, jeering, and scuffling — have no counterpart in Mexico. There was rather an air of deferential, quiet curiosity. Owing to the large number present, it was decided to hold the meeting in the yard. There were no seats except for Jesus and myself, and the crowd stood about or sat upon the ground. But the utmost endeavors of El Pajaro failed to bring them close to us. Whatever the reason, they kept as far away as the limits of the yard permitted, leaving before us a considerable space untenanted. I expected this would embarrass Jesus, but it didn't. He spoke easily, pleasantly, familiarly. He caught their attention, aroused their interest and held it. I could understand enough to know he was telling the old, sweet story of Bethlehem. Every face was softened in sympathy. He told of the carpenter's son, dutiful and industrious, living so like themselves, His simple, lowly life. Then the Christ, healing the sick, raising the dead, giving to men the new Gospel of doing unto others as they would be done by. Last, that sacrifice sublime on Calvary! There were

grave faces and glistening eyes. This sacrifice
was for them; for them this God had come on
earth and died. Such was Christianity. That
same Christ who died on Calvary, lived in Heaven,
looking down upon them and asking them to come
to Him. He was there for all. He did not require that they seek Him in confessional. He did
not ask that they come with a priest. The sinner
had but to will and be saved.

I imagined that all present being Catholics,
some might resent this reflection on their clergy or
creed. But there was no sign of resentment. They
continued attentive, respectful, and were even
seemingly convinced. Clearly, great results could
be counted on, for Jesus had simply led up to a
commanding position and was unlimbering his
heaviest guns for an assault on Rome. But an
untoward incident occurred. At either side of the
yard was tethered a rooster, the only ones left of a
large number which El Pajaro had bred for the
ring. Whether by their own efforts or by the aid
of some mischievous pelados, the birds became
freed from their bonds, and with elongated necks
stealthily sought each other. They met in the
open space in front of us. Jesus kept on as if
unconscious of the counter attraction, but it was
too much. Nobody heard the minister — every

eye was on the roosters. Those who sat stood up, those who were standing moved forward. A solid circle was formed, and the battle was on. The birds spurred and picked. There were cheers of encouragement. Bets were called. Even with El Pajaro, love for the national sport overleapt zeal for his new-found faith, and he shouted a bet on the black : —

"Valedores!" he cried. "Voy cinco pesos al negro!" ("I'll bet five dollars on the black!")

We walked away unnoticed. Jesus did not speak for several minutes, and when he did it was to remark that he thought El Pajaro would lose his bet.

CHAPTER XXIV

THERE is no telling how rich a harvest might
have been reaped in Alameda, had the season of
religious fervor run a natural course. Spiritual
progress was beyond all precedent. The Institute,
of course, was in the forefront of the movement,
but other missions participated. Not to be out-
done by the Reverend Lamb, three branch missions were started by the Reverend Tuttle, two by
Reverend Josh, and other sects hastily sent forward their reapers and gleaners. Each of these
joined with the Reverend Lamb in the fight against
Rome, and at the same time they wrestled for souls
with each other. Hardly a street that did not echo
nightly to good old revival airs sung with Spanish
words. Jesus carried the war to the very citadel
of the enemy by holding meetings opposite the
Cathedral. No wonder weird tales went out when
the bats, disturbed by such unusual sounds, filled
the dark edifice with their cries and flights. Fat

priests were said to be scowling from the belfry windows. The Reverend Lamb saw them, and told me how they were being consumed with impotent rage. I saw two of them that same night seated together in the Cathedral yard. I could not say they were being consumed — they were certainly smoking.

But when everything looked most favorable, there came a blight — politics. The public mind, that had been cultivated in the light and warmth needful to the growth of religious ideas, became superheated with the excitement of a political campaign. The sprouts of the new faith were choked with the weeds of partisanship.

It was as unexpected as untimely. An election in Mexico, local or national, is, as a rule, the merest perfunctory ceremony. The effort of good citizens is always to avoid friction and make any sacrifice for the sake of peace. But occasionally harmony is impossible. The arts of intrigue, the play of ambition, force some one to the front who is utterly obnoxious.

Such was the case in the candidacy of Benavides. If half that was said of him were true, he was more deserving of the penitentiary than the State House, stripes rather than laurels. He had, so it was said, maltreated his parents, swindled his nearest kindred, defrauded widows and orphans, violated every trust. But strange to say, the strongest charge against him, and that which at once accounted for his enemies and friends, was that he was the subservient tool of the priests.

For there are two chief parties in Mexico, by whatever names they are known, the Clerical or "Conservadores," and the anti-Clerical or "Liberales." Benavides belonged to the former. So did Governor Romero, but not pronouncedly; he was a conservative man, respected even by his partisan opponents, while his prospective son-in-law was believed to represent all that was pernicious and offensive in priestcraft. Thus it was that the usual quiet of a prearranged succession was disturbed with violent contention. The opposition, at first the merest mutterings of protest, grew louder and bolder; meetings were held, clubs formed, leaders chosen. The agitation extended to all classes, and soon reached those with whom the Reverend Lamb and his colleagues were laboring. Alas! the evil of it. How could prayer and sermon and song contend against flare of fireworks, the blare of bands, the wild whoops of factions, the noise and excitement and glory of parades! One by one the missions closed — Tuttle first, then Josh, even the Reverend Lamb at last withdrew from the unequal struggle. A wretch had arisen in a prayer meeting as if to pray, but, instead, began a fierce political harangue, and those who had been praying and singing not only listened, but broke forth in ungodly demonstrations of approval.

Of all the evangelists Jesus alone maintained the fight with marvellous pluck. Every other mission closed — his still kept open. He would not give up. But the attendance dwindled and drooped. It was discouraging. Men in whose complete regeneracy he had prided, abandoned him, even El Pajaro. Women in the middle of a fervent period or touching hymn would leap away at the first toot of a brass band. Twice he changed his place of meeting where he thought he would be remote from political turmoil. But as if by sheer malice some Club would start in his immediate neighborhood.

One evening I attended and found him sorely depressed. A passing procession had emptied the room during his evening prayer. Miss Anderson was playing the organ and singing at the time, and to her credit be it said, notwithstanding the desertion, calmly proceeded with every verse. At the close of her song we consulted. Jesus was for giving up. She held out for going on.

"I can never stand another such experience," he said.

She answered in her deep, decisive tone: "Leave that to me. We will meet here on Wednesday night."

CHAPTER XXV

WEDNESDAY night came, and with it most unpropitious signs for the success of Miss Anderson's meeting. A great rally announced for the plaza! A new speaker coming from another town and two big parades! I could hear the din of gathering crowds as I left the hotel, and saw ever and anon the flash of soaring rockets.

" No Mexican, man or woman, will be away from the plaza to-night," thought I. But to my amazement and great joy when I entered the little mission room more people were in attendance than for many a day, and more were still coming. Even before the hour of opening, the place was filled. On the face of Jesus as he rose for prayer there was a glow of thanksgiving and pride.

Not only did the people come, they staid to the end. Once in the middle of the service I heard afar the music of an approaching band. It came and passed, but scarcely one of his audience heeded it. Miss Anderson bore a look of triumph. Jesus was jubilant.

"How did you do it ?" he asked.

"Where there's a will there's a way," she answered.

"Miss Anderson is a wonderful woman," said I, on the way home.

"She is indeed," he replied, and it was the first time any of my references to her was received by him with enthusiasm.

"A fit mate for an evangelist," he went on; "with her energy, zeal, and resources what might be accomplished ? "

This was so much in line with the wishes of the Reverend Lamb that I was not surprised at the high spirits of the latter the next time we met.

"There may be a wedding at the Institute yet," said he, prodding me jocularly with his forefinger. I must have looked as if I thought the act unclerical, for he clasped his hands, raised his eyes, and added, "If the Lord so wills it."

The next meeting under the management of Miss Anderson was still more notable. It not only filled the small room, but many were on the sidewalk clamoring for admittance. Indeed, so violent became the pious zeal of those outside to get in that a policeman had to be summoned to keep order. What made this great attendance particularly gratifying was the fact of a political meeting the same night only a couple of squares away. The Lord was with us.

After service our hearts were so glad we held a thanksgiving at the Institute. Miss Anderson was the heroine. The Reverend Lamb praised her in his prayer as one whom God had singled out for this special work. Nos. 1, 2, and 3 paid her appropriate tribute, and Jesus closed with a fervent invocation of further blessings on their joint labors, at which the Reverend Lamb ejaculated a loud and significant "Amen!" Things were going his way. Was I pleased or not? I could not say. But when Jesus came to the hotel next morning looking nervous, excited, and embarrassed, and told me that he wanted my counsel in a personal matter of great moment, it threw me into a panic.

"Let us take a walk," said I, hastily; "my head aches." And out we started. At the door we were stopped by an old woman who gave Jesus a letter. He looked puzzled when he read it, and asked her a question to which she responded volubly. Her answer seemed to confound him and he stood staring at her.

"What is the matter?" I asked. He handed me the letter. It was as follows:—

PAROQUIA DE LA SANTISSIMA TRINIDAD.

Por la presente certifico que la portadora, Guadalupe Varela, es una mujer honrada y puedo recomendarla como veridica y honesta.

PABLO MOREL, Cura Parroco.

"It is a certificate from the priest, Pablo Morel, that this woman is of good character and truthful," explained Jesus.

"And what business has she with you?"

He hesitated a moment, then replied:—

"She claims that she was promised a medio [six and one-fourth cents] for herself and for each one she would bring to our meeting last night; that she came there and brought her husband and six children, but could not get in on account of the crowd. She claims fifty cents."

"Who promised to pay her for going to meeting?"

Jesus hesitated, hung his head, looked uneasy and troubled, but finally answered,—

"She says it was Miss Anderson."

I at once suspected fraud.

"Ask her why she got a letter from a priest to help her in the matter. What has the priest to do with it?" said I.

" Porque fue Vd. al Sacerdote en este negocio ? "
Jesus asked.

It was the woman's turn to look troubled. With
evident embarrassment she replied : —

" Antes de ir a la reunion pedi permiso al Padre
y me dijo que estaba bien siempre que le diera la
mitad para la Iglesia. Todos los demas hicieron
lo mismo."

The face of Jesus was pallid and his voice faltered as he translated : —

" She says that she asked the priest's permission
to attend the meeting, and he gave permission pro-
viding she would pay him half the proceeds for
the church. All the others, she says, did the
same."

" Well, I'll be —. But there must be some
mistake. Go with her at once to Miss Anderson."

He left with her while I sat down to ponder on
the devious ways of mission work in Mexico.

I expected him back shortly, for we had agreed
on a stroll together. But he did not come. After
a full hour a boy brought a note from him which
read : —

The woman's story is true.

JESUS.

*　　*　　*　　*　　*

That afternoon I chanced to meet Mrs. Lamb,
who, followed by Antonio with a bundle, was on

her customary round. I joined her and saw her leave in nearly every hut we visited, some little article of need, — a child's dress, a pair of shoes, a cake of soap, or a doll, — yes! for one old toothless creature a big package of cigarettes. And when I caught the gleam of joy that greeted her coming, and the glow of gratitude that blessed her going, I wondered if after all her way is not the best. Certainly the Reverend Lamb should make more of her in his Reports.

CHAPTER XXVI

JESUS IN POLITICS

In the weak, spiritless state that follows failure, one is apt to yield easily to the first influence, be the same good or bad. So it was with Jesus. His boyhood's dream, the sole ambition of his youth, the loyal faith of manhood, was the spiritual uplifting of his race. For this alone he lived, and all his life had prayed and planned. Whirled off for a while by a sudden wave of passion, the revival had drawn him back and fixed anew his holy purpose. Then the occasion came; he seized it and was borne aloft upon the luminous wings of hope and faith. He had reached at last an exalted plane that seemed in very sight of his cherished goal, when fate dashed him down. He felt himself worse than a failure — a laughing-stock. For who would hear of those subsidized meetings and not make him the butt of gibe and scorn? Day after day I met him, but he turned from me dumb and desolate. He wanted to be alone, and the Reverend Lamb and I, gloomy ourselves over the sudden collapse of the mission movement, made the grave mistake of thinking it would be better so. We left him to himself. Others, however, sought him.

By some mischance there had passed from tongue to tongue the story of his duel with Benavides. Enemies of the latter made it a dramatic tale, in which Benavides was the baffled villain and Jesus the chivalric hero. On the very day succeeding the dreadful revelation regarding Miss Anderson's meetings, a laudatory letter came to him at the Institute. Many such followed. Men whom he did not know stopped him in the street and embraced him. Little groups gathered as he passed, and cheered. Within a week he had drunk the wine of popularity. Before Reverend Lamb or myself was aware, he was in consultation with the moving spirits of the political campaign, nay, an actual attendant at their meetings. Craig first informed me of this; but I saw at once how it had come about.

Of course I took him to task for it and strove to impress him with the utter impropriety of one of his calling mixing in such business. But he insisted that it was his duty. "Benavides is a villain, an oppressor of the poor, a tool of the priests," he declared.

"And the accepted lover of Señorita Romero," I added to myself.

The Reverend Lamb, I discovered, was also opposed to Benavides, whom he believed to be a hireling of the Vatican.

"It would be a bad thing," he said, "for the future of missionary work to have such a man governor." But he counselled Jesus against any indiscretion.

Now I abhor the mixing of religion and politics. I have seen much of it at home, and never have known other than evil to come from it. In my judgment, the Reverend Lamb should have forbidden, positively forbidden, Jesus from taking any part in the matter, publicly or privately. Admitting that Rome was in it, if Rome saw fit to run Benavides, let her. That is natural in Rome, but our church is above such business, far above it. Missionaries particularly, I argued, should avoid political intrigue. They are permitted to pursue their sacred work by the tolerance of the law of the land and under the protection of its constituted authorities, and it is no business of theirs to make or unmake them. Reverend Lamb agreed to all this with some reservations. Jesus, however, quite promptly rejoined that although he was a missionary, he was at the same time a Mexican; that his duties to his church did not absolve him from his duties to his country. I couldn't gainsay this. He was doubtless sincere, yet I felt in my bones that if it wasn't for a certain señorita, he would regard very differently his relative duties to church and state. Passion colors the conscience of the best of us.

My protests were of no avail. He spoke at meetings, appeared at a public parade, and was chosen chairman of a club. His erratic, fierce energies were transferred from the fight against Rome to the fight against Benavides.

"He is overdoing it," said the Reverend Lamb. "Out till midnight every night and often away from his duties during the day. I can stand much, very much, but there is a point at which patience ceases to be a virtue." This was said ominously.

I seldom saw him. Once he passed the hotel mounted on a spirited horse and dressed in a cavalier "charro" costume. At another time I met him distributing what I supposed to be tracts, but subsequently found to be political handbills. In fact, he developed an aptitude for politics that showed unerringly the Irish origin of his grandfather.

CHAPTER XXVII

YET I must admit that his brief discourse one Sunday afternoon at the joint service of the English-speaking residents of Alameda, was most exemplary, breathing fervent piety and full of good sense. We were all proud of him. It was evidence of the grand work which could be accomplished with his priest-ridden countrymen. "Indeed" (as Brother Lamb said in the closing prayer), " had it not been for the Institute and the spirit that fostered it, this inspired young man to whom we have just listened might be among the poor creatures we see to-day gathered on the hill worshipping the Virgin Mary."

The Reverend Lamb was referring to a sort of festival then taking place on a hill near Alameda, which had attracted thousands of the poorer classes. After the service that afternoon I went up to look at the crowd out of curiosity. Most of them were apparently sight-seers like myself. But round a huge cross were kneeling fully a thousand mot-

ley-costumed men and women, and the strange
murmur of their prayers made a weird sound.
There was no priest among them, and I was told
that the priests discountenanced the ceremony.
But the masses clung to it.   The monotonous praying soon wearied me and I was about to leave,
when suddenly they rose from their knees and
began to circle around the cross.   Then a sort of
chant was started in which all soon joined, keeping
time with an uncouth dance.   I had seen just such
a dance in Northern Wisconsin and in the Dakotas,
and by the very same sort of people.   Catholics?
you ask.   No! Indians.   For these poor wretches
who sang and leaped about the cross were nothing
else, only of a darker type than those we are accustomed to, and that wild song had been sung,
and that grotesque dance had been danced possibly a thousand years before Christ came on
earth.   Yet I did not doubt, as I looked and
listened, that had the True Faith been given a
chance, it would long since have wrought a change
to better things.   It did not occur to me that the
True Faith had had the chance in the places I mentioned, in New England, Wisconsin, and the Dakotas.   I simply thought of Jesus Delaney and what
was done for him.   Not that he would have been
cavorting around that cross in any event,—his

family were not of that class, — but beyond any doubt he would have been confessing to priests, prostrating himself before images, worshipping the Virgin, and indulging in all ·the debasing superstitions of his people. Whatever his faults, he was done with that forever. But it was too bad that other weaknesses were not eradicated.

Somebody has written that the education of a child should begin twenty years before it is born. Whoever wrote that may have had some such acquaintance as Jesus. I will go further in his case and say it would have been well if his education had begun with his Irish, Spanish, and Indian ancestry. I would not then have had the humiliation of seeing him that very night — but I must tell it.

Weary from my long walk up the hill and down, instead of going to the plaza Sunday evening, I sat resting in front of the hotel. It was an odd procession which kept passing. Now a scattering squad of soldiers, each armed with a long stick of sugar-cane which he ravenously chewed and expectorated, then groups of gorgeously dressed señoritas highly powdered and strongly scented, on their way to the plaza, anon a drove of dwarfed donkeys laden with bundles of wood bigger than themselves, beggars of all sorts and

conditions of whining misery, cocheros urging
starved-looking horses with lash and shout, song-
ful caballeros, — drunk and sober,— policemen, big
and little (mostly little and miserably uniformed),
with prisoners, — one officer oftentimes to three
maudlin offenders, three or four officers sometimes
required for one, — I counted sixty such wretches
in an hour, the last being Antonio with a policeman at his head, another at his feet, borne proudly
by shouting as he passed, " Viva Mexico ! "

Presently there was a great commotion. Vehicles turned up side streets, promenaders fled into
hallways, even officers and soldiers took fright and
flight. Coming down the street at full speed on
horses wild and foaming was a party of madmen,
firing their pistols in a perfect fusillade and shriek-
ing : " Abajo Benavides ! Muera Benavides ! "
(Down with Benavides ! Death to Benavides !)
The foremost of the gang was Jesus.

CHAPTER XXVIII

EL CLUB PROGRESIVO POLITICO, or the Progressive Political Club of which Jesus was President, was in serious straits for money. In its zeal for the cause of Reform, debts had been incurred without provision for their payment, and many of these were being pressed by creditors. So at the regular weekly meeting following the patriotic demonstration described in the preceding chapter, the matter of raising funds was earnestly considered. Various plans were discussed, but that which met with most favor was the motion of Señor Don Calixto Santa Maria, called El Profesor, (he taught ethics in the College of "La Purisima,") that the Club give a bull-fight. The only objection urged against it, was the prevailing high price of fighting bulls, and this was more than offset by the low price of horses, three or four of which would likely be gored to death on the occasion. Doubtless the motion of El Profesor would have been unanimously carried, had it not been that Jesus

made a strong speech against bull-fighting generally and the proposed exhibition in particular.
So earnest and eloquent his protest, and such the
influence he had acquired, that a substitute submitted by El Pajaro was adopted. Instead of a
bull-fight, it was decided to have a booth at the
coming fiesta and devote the proceeds thereof to
the Club treasury.

Jesus was elated with this moral victory, and
told me all the details as we went together to
the fiesta on the opening night.

"It shows, notwithstanding their love for the
national sport," said he, "my countrymen are
open to reason."

(This from a man whom I had vainly tried to
convince of the impropriety of firing pistols in the
street as an assertion of political opinion!)

Neither of us had been to a fiesta, but we read
in the Governor's proclamation in the official
journal of Alameda that it was the annual cele-
bration or fair, chartered by the state legislature,
"for the promotion of the arts and industry and
the interchange of foreign and domestic commod-
ities." The proclamation further recited "that
order should be maintained, peace and security
to property guaranteed, and that only such games
not prohibited by law would be allowed."

We found a vast crowd in attendance. A band played, and the people promenaded as at the plaza, or patronized the booths, of which there were no less than fifty. After looking awhile at the interesting concourse, we started to find the booth of the Progressive Political Club. I had expected from the official proclamation, as did Jesus, that the booths would be devoted to exhibits of art and manufacture, or some sort of light traffic or entertainment. But the first we entered was taken up with a long table, at which men and women sat playing Spanish Monte. The next booth differed from the first by having two tables instead of one. The next was a saloon in full blast, and the next and still another were gambling dens. We entered no more, for as we passed along in search of the Club, each successive booth warned us of its business by the clink of glasses or the rattle of chips.

Our search was in vain. Not only did we fail to find the Club booth, but stranger still not a member known to Jesus was anywhere visible. We wandered about watching with much disfavor the little outside stands, each of which had some penny-catching game of chance. Here an old woman with a pack of cards, there an old man with a dice-box, the stake a penny,

N

the bank an ostentatious heap of pennies, the gamesters children. Yet officers of the law looked on! We happened at last to pass a booth from which came a voice both of us at once recognized as that of El Pajaro. He was calling in a sing-song way:—

"Por aca! Por aca! Aqui esta la suerte! Con uno ganan treinta seis! El doce colorado! Otra vez va la bola! El cobarde que nada arriesga nada gana! Vengan por aca! Aqui esta la suerte!" (Come here! Come here! Here's your luck! Thirty-six for one! Twelve red! Once more goes the ball, etc.)

We entered; it was the booth of "El Club Progresivo Politico." It contained a long table, round which sat a number of members and a fair proportion of non-members, among whom was my friend Craig. In a hollow in the centre of the table a nickel-plated wheel whirled with a series of numbers, while a little ivory ball rolled in the opposite direction. On each side was a large green cloth with the corresponding numbers of the wheel in red and black figures. It was roulette, and the dealer was El Pajaro. Entirely unabashed, he gave us a quick nod of recognition and kept up his sing-song: "Aqui esta la suerte! Todo parejo! Todo limpio! Aqui esta la fortuna!" and he deftly whirled the tempting wheel.

I did not dare to look at Jesus. I felt that his mortification must be unbearable. The Club of which he was President, carrying on a wretched catch-penny gambling game! The convert of whom he was so proud publicly playing the rôle of a common gambler! But when at last I turned to leave, what was my surprise to see no sign of shame or sorrow. On the contrary, he seemed absorbed in the play, and eager as El Pajaro himself that the bank should win. He followed the whirling ball round and round. Now it fell in a number which paid Craig 28 for 1, and his countenance clouded; now it dropped into the spot marked with a double cipher, which swept every penny wagered into the coffer of El Pajaro, and he rubbed his hands gleefully.

"This is no place for a clergyman," I whispered. "Let us go."

"No? Why not?" he answered. "What's—" then as if startled with a sudden sense of its impropriety he shook his head regretfully.

"You are right," he said. "Let us go," and we went out.

I resolved to read him a lesson on the evil consequences of bad company.

"You see, Jesus," I began, placing my hand on his shoulder, "you see —" but he stopped, unheeding me, and followed with rapt gaze a figure among the promenaders.   It was Señorita Romero.

He stood transfixed.   Several times she passed us, but not once did she chance to catch his eager, worshipful eyes.   Presently, with her escort, an aged lady, she entered a booth.   Without a word we followed.   There sat Señorita Romero playing roulette.

*   *   *   *   *

Whether it was the precedent set by his adored, or just such a calculation as I confess to myself, and which made winning a mathematical certainty, — whatever the cause, a few minutes after Miss Romero's departure found Jesus in the seat she had occupied, with a stack of chips before him, feverishly staking every turn of the wheel.

CHAPTER XXIX

JESUS GOES TO SANTA ROSA

THE story of the riotous ride had already reached the Reverend Lamb. Then came a dark tale of gambling at the fiesta. That settled it. Even Miss Anderson admitted Jesus should leave the Institute. Not that the incident created any particular comment among the Mexicans. It didn't. The appearance of a clergyman at a game of lawn tennis would be scarcely more remarkable with us. But rival missions were concerned. The Reverend Josh and the Reverend Tuttle were both greatly shocked. To them it was a gross scandal — a scandal which would militate against the further spread of the Gospel. They reported it to their respective Boards; they deplored it to their respective congregations; they even went so far as to join in a protest to the Reverend Lamb. Within a week there came from the Executive Board a peremptory order for the transfer of Jesus to Santa Rosa. It was a wretched affair all around, and the worst phase of it was the seeming blindness of Jesus to any sense of wrong-doing. He showed no regret, no repentance. When told of the order of the Board, he rebelled. He informed the Reverend Lamb that he would either remain at the Institute or quit the ministry. He informed Miss Anderson that he was master of his own conscience, and that she should be satisfied to be mistress of hers. But his temper softened after a brief appeal from Mrs. Lamb. "For my sake, Jesus," she pleaded. "There are three hundred souls at Santa Rosa. They know not God. Fathers and mothers there who live in darkness. You can bring the light. There are little children who have never heard of Christ. Go to them, Jesus." "I will go," he said impulsively. But when the Reverend Lamb held out his hand in pious approbation, he gave a contemptuous toss of the head and turned aside.

I was at the depot to bid him good-by. I talked encouragingly of his new field and the great good he could accomplish. He would be happy in the work.

He never answered, but looked at me with such mournful remonstrance that I stopped. A few moments before the train pulled out, a queer, squatty figure surmounted by a high and wide-brimmed hat approached us. I recognized Antonio.

"Yo tambien voy con Usted, Don Jesus," he said.   He was asking to be taken along.

"No, Antonio, impossible, no puedes venir conmigo."

The wrinkled old face began to work convulsively and was soon wet with tears.

"Yo tambien voy," he said. "Yo tambien voy," he repeated, just as a crying child whose heart was obstinately set on something. "Su madre quiere que me vaya con Usted." Then he changed instantly to an air of cheerful confidence.

"Aqui esta la Señora," and turning, we saw the mother of Jesus.

She too pleaded, urging him to take Antonio.

"Llevate a Antonio, Jesus," she said.   He drew her gently aside and reasoned with her, but she had her way.   Before the final bell struck for departure, I saw the face of Antonio grinning happily at the window of a second-class car.

"If I don't get up to see you in a week or so, Jesus, write to me," I said.   I bade him good-by and the train glided away.

I had become attached to the young man, yet I felt a great relief when he was gone.   It would put an end to the untoward happenings which, while brought about by no intent of mine, were somehow so closely coincident I

could not help feeling a sort of responsibility.
My conscience acquitted me of any wrong in the
matter. I reasoned it over again and again and
always with that result, yet still would come a
qualm of feeling that but for me, Jesus would never
have had such experiences and would still have
been in the undisturbed sanctity of routine work at
the Institute. But nothing more could happen
because of me now. He was gone and I ought
to be glad of it. Yet while there was, as I say,
a sense of relief, there was with it a feeling of regret, and this last feeling strengthened day by day.
I missed him. There was a charm in his companionship indescribable. Craig was far better posted
than he on Mexican affairs, and the Reverend
Lamb was certainly better informed upon mission
work, yet I spent little time in the society of either
that I did not yearn for Jesus. Somehow he
brought back to me vividly the fulness and fresh-
ness of my own youth. Or was it that while with
him, and even away from him, there often rose in
my mind a notion which almost became a belief,
that the little one for whom the mother gave her
life at birth, and whom I laid at her side within a
week, would have grown like him. He would have
—Yes, sir. They were all big, comely men on his
mother's side, and the men of my people were all

larger, better looking, more athletic than myself, and he was a likely baby, straight-limbed, broad-chested, sweet-faced.   Had he lived — well —

I watched for a letter from Jesus, and when finally one came, I was almost ashamed of my nervous eagerness for news of him.   I didn't even wait to reach my room, but at once opened the envelope and to my intense disappointment drew out a smaller one sealed and addressed : —

SEÑORITA MARIE ROMERO,
Alameda, Mexico.

Was there nothing for me?   No word?   Yes. Peering into the open envelope, I found a little, forlorn scrap of paper on which was scrawled : —

I know you will deliver this.
JESUS.

I was so indignant, I could have torn scrap and all into shreds.   If the fellow had only deigned to tell me something of himself, how he was, what he was doing.   But to thrust on me the devious work of carrying his correspondence — to make me a go-between!   What did he take me for? No!   I am not that sort of a man.   But I resisted the first impulse to tear the thing, and simply decided to send back to Jesus the sealed envelope, and decline with dignity the office he saw fit to

assign me.   I went to my room and began a letter
to him.   But I got calmer as I wrote, and reflected
that I must not say anything to hurt the poor lad's
feelings.   Finally I stopped writing and my eyes
caught the words of that little, plaintive scrawl:
"I know you will deliver this.   Jesus."   He knew
I would.   He knew me better, it seemed, than I
knew myself, for I tore up the unfinished letter,
and rose from my desk with a determination to
convey his missive to Miss Romero.

CHAPTER XXX

BUT how was I to do so? I had not met her
nor her father since the dinner party. I had no
reasonable excuse for seeing either of them now.
Besides, she might be away. There was real relief
in this last possibility. But I set about my task.
Now, with an American girl, such a mission would
involve no trouble; a special delivery stamp, and
the nearest mail-box. But in Mexico, young
ladies don't get letters by mail, nor do they re-
ceive gentlemen callers, young or old. They are
watched and guarded as if home were a convent
and every man a designing monster. How was
I to give that letter to Miss Romero? I couldn't
stalk the plaza like a love-struck fool, and hand
it to her as I passed. I couldn't prowl about her
house or play " tick-tack-toe " at her window. Of
course I might bribe a servant. But could I be
sure of the servant? What certainty was there
that the servant would not take my bribe and the

letter to Governor Romero?   It was all in all a miserable business.   But fortune favored me.

Walking along the street, my mind muddled by a throng of utterly irrational ways and means of delivering surreptitious letters, I came to the Cathedral.   Here I paused, as was my custom, to gaze at the stately structure.   Just then a carriage drew up, and as luck would have it who should alight and enter the church but Miss Romero.   "There," thought I, "is the one place she can go unattended.   Yet it is the one place where communication with her would be grossly improper."   Without definite purpose, I walked in after her and watched her go to a pew near the great altar and adjoining a confessional.   I stood a moment irresolute, then went up the long aisle and entered the pew immediately behind her. She was kneeling.   I did the same.   It was my first show of devotion in a Catholic church; but God knows my motive was not idolatrous, so the act may be forgiven me.   Still I could not help thinking the shock it would have given the Reverend Lamb, Miss Anderson, or my good friends at home had any of them come upon me in such an attitude in such a place.

Miss Romero, while she knelt, read from a dainty, plush-bound prayer-book.   Presently the curtains of the confessional parted, a penitent emerged and Miss Romero closed her book, laid it down, and entered the vacant apartment. The moment the curtains closed behind her, I stealthily reached to the little book, inserted the letter of Jesus, and resumed my devotions.

No wretch who had just picked a pocket, no burglar still on the plundered premises could feel more apprehension. I imagined the priest scowling at me from the confessional. I felt keen eyes glaring from every side. I seemed to hear the murmur of voices telling of the sacrilege. I was seized with actual terror. Yet I held my ground nor moved until the click of the closing slide and the silken rustle told me Miss Romero had finished.

Now was the critical moment.

I almost held my breath. I looked anxiously at the beautiful face lit up with sanctity, but downcast lids veiled the eyes. She reëntered her pew, knelt, prayed awhile, then reached down and got her prayer-book. I saw the slight sensitive body shudder and the lovely head fall forward. My dread became intolerable. Had she fainted? No! Thank God. Her head raised again with an audible sigh. I kept my kneeling posture. I knew that my limbs were trembling. It seemed to me a long, long time, but finally she rose.   As she passed, our eyes met and the look in hers was certainly not resentment.

On leaving that Catholic church, I made a solemn vow never to enter another on any such mission.

Seated in front of the hotel in the evening, thinking over what had occurred, an elderly woman dressed in black accosted me.   She held up an envelope, inquiring if it was for me : —

"Sera esto para Usted, Señor?"

"Si, Señora," I answered, observing my name.

She handed it to me and walked away.

Opening the envelope, I found within another, sealed and addressed : —

SR. DON JESUS DELANEY.

Unfolded beside it lay a tiny strip, which read :—

Suplico mande entregar a su destino, favor que mucho agredecera, Su Attente Servidora,

M. R.

I was in for it again.   M. R. was doubtless Marie Romero, and she, too, had appointed me her postman.

CHAPTER XXXI

MY RIDE TO SANTA ROSA

THE next day I started for Santa Rosa.

"It is a ride of one hundred miles by rail and eighteen more by wagon," said the conductor of whom I made inquiry.

"Can I reach there in good season to-night?"

"Yes, if you are lucky enough to catch the stage at Barotera and get through unmolested."

"Unmolested! Is there any danger?"

"Well, there have been tricks upon travellers of late between Barotera and Santa Rosa. The stage was stopped and robbed two weeks ago, and a few days since the pay wagon was looted."

"Anybody hurt?"

"Yes, two or three shot."

"But the authorities?"

"Oh, the authorities are active enough. The Rurales are scouring the whole district and killing every suspect."

"Killing every suspect! You don't mean that the accused in such cases are not given a trial?"

" Just what I mean.   The ' Ley contra Bandidos, Plagiaros y Salteadores,' and the ' Ley Fuga ' give the necessary authority.   And under those laws, which I must say are prompt and effective, the Rurales simply exterminate the bad characters in any locality where such an outrage occurs."

" But are the men not given a hearing?   Are they not first identified ? "

" Well, yes, and the law provides 'that after identification the culprits be summarily executed.' But the commander easily settles this little detail in his report to headquarters after his return to town."

" If they have done so in this instance there should be no danger now between Barotera and Santa Rosa."

" I suppose not, but somehow people are timid for a time."

Here was a condition in my journey I had not anticipated, and it gave me some uneasiness.   My anxiety was increased when on reaching Barotera I found that the regular stage would not run that evening.

" El sol baja antes de las seis," said the stage agent, " y habria tres horas de camino sin siquiera luna."   (The sun sets before six, and there will be three hours without a moon.)

"But, pero, there is no danger — no peligro; the Rurales are here — estan aqui," I said.

"Si." He gave a shrug that seemed to say there will be less danger when the Rurales are gone.

Now I did not come to remain in Barotera over night. I had heard from Craig of the discomforts of such a stopping-place, bad food, foul bed, and worse bedfellows. So I determined to hire a vehicle and driver. I offered the usual fare — "No, Señor!" emphatically No. "Double" — "No, Señor," but rather reluctantly No. "Treble" — My offer was accepted, and soon I was whirling along a very good though dusty road on the way to Santa Rosa.

The view was a noble one. At either hand the level plain carpet covered with mesquite made a vast stage. To the west the blazing sun as it hung low lit up the whole vast range of broken gorges and spiral peaks, making a sublime tableau. Now the sun balanced on an illuminated ridge, now it seemed to squat and swell, growing redder and fiercer as if its anger would consume the universe. It did not set; it burned into the mountains and left the flare and flame of a mighty conflagration. I bathed my soul in the glory of it.

Almost while the dazzle of the god of day was

o

yet blinding the eye, the mountains shot forth baneful shades. These deepening, darkening black — the night came down. Elation vanished with the light. In its stead came a keen accusing sense of my fool's errand. Where was I going? I knew not. What for? I could not say. But this much was plain. I was alone at night in a region infested by robbers. The dull whirl of the wheels, the tramp of the horses' hoofs, the hiss of the constant whip, the queer cries of the driver, made the ever gathering darkness more uncanny.

"Uicha! uicha! arri! arri! Anden brutos, . . . cuelen flojos . . . upha! upha bestias! . . . arri — arri uicha! . . ." On we went — the same jarring monotony of wheels, hoofs, whip, and jargon.

"Aqui, Señor, aqui," said my driver, turning suddenly, "aqui la diligencia fue robada y dos pasajeros perdieron la vida." (Here, sir, here the stage was robbed and two passengers lost their lives.) His beady eyes gleamed and his white teeth glistened. "Uicha! uicha! arri! arri!" — on we went. The night was now a deep into which we seemed to plunge. A strange fear took possession of me. Some premonition — call it what you will — made me rise. There was a shot, a wild shout, and in an instant our horses were seized and all about were mounted men, flourishing pistols and looking ferociously desperate and murderous.

"Madre de Dios!" exclaimed the driver, dropping his lines and falling on his knees.

There was no hope of resistance. So, believing that he knew the proper behavior for such a crisis, I too knelt, holding up my hands.

The leader came close and asked me a question. I did not understand him. He repeated it more peremptorily, making it still less intelligible. I saw he was getting angry. "Responde," he demanded sternly. "Estoy Americano," I shouted. "No can hablo your lingo — I mean lengua Español." He turned and spoke to the driver, whose eyes at first rolled, then steadied, then stared, and his tongue at last loosened. Such a torrent as came! And as it flowed he seemed to gain courage, lowering his hands, rising from his knees, coolly regaining his lines, and at last whirling his whip and striking his horses, away we went. I could not protest. I could only crouch low where I knelt, expecting every instant the leaden death. Presently I felt the hand of the driver pulling at my shoulder, and as I looked up he spoke:—

"Rurales! Señor, son los Rurales." (Rurales! Sir, they are Rurales.)

The supposed bandits were officers of the law searching the locality.

I resumed my seat, nor uttered a word, but dark as it was I could see the burly body of that driver shaking, and hear ever and anon above the whirl and prance and lash, the coarse chuckle of his laughter. "Uicha! uicha! arri! arri!" On we went, laboring heavily up steep courses, still in the blank of darkness. Mile after mile, the very seconds dragging with the crunching wheels, and still impenetrable, soulless darkness. Again I felt the creeping chill of fear, the sense of impending danger. There was a quick check to our ascent. The horses reared, then stood shuddering. What was coming? Suddenly as from heaven, yet so near as to be startling, there fell on my ears a deep, full baritone voice singing in English:—

> "And 'twas from Aunt Dinah's quilting party
> I was seeing Nelly home."

Then came a chorus, just such a young, strong, hearty chorus as we used to give at Annapolis:—

> "I was seeing Nelly home,
> I was seeing Nelly home,
> It was from Aunt Dinah's quilting party
> I was seeing Nelly home."

"Americanos," said the driver, grinning.

Ay, thank God, those were American voices! No mistaking that; and in the glory of that swelling chorus the darkness and my fear were lifted.

A few minutes, and several thousand dogs were making noisy announcement of our arrival in Santa Rosa.

CHAPTER XXXII

A JOLLY PARTY

WE inquired for the Reverend Jesus Delaney. He was with "Los Americanos." I should have known it. Who, with any heart, within a radius of a mile could have helped being drawn into that chorus? It was ringing out yet, louder, fuller, each young voice giving a fresh verse, each doubtless having his own idea of Nelly and the party from which he was seeing her home. As our vehicle drew up in front of the long, low portico where the singers sat, I was joining in with all my strength of lung, so that it happened when, surprised by our arrival, the chorus stopped short, I maintained my part good and strong to the end, proclaiming to the very stars " I was seeing Nelly home."

Jesus ran out to welcome me. There was an eager inquiry in face and eyes that I at once sought to relieve by delivering the little missive with which I had been intrusted. He kissed it passionately, and without a word disappeared in the darkness. I had to introduce myself to the group, who greeted me cordially.

"It is written in the charter," said one, "that every American who visits Santa Rosa must spend his first night here."

When Jesus returned, his face lit up with supreme happiness, he found me on good terms with all, and indeed their guest. It was the house of the Superintendent of the mine, built on a narrow ledge overlooking the village. With him lived his two brothers, and also the company doctor and foreman (none of them over thirty years of age), and two visiting friends, as jolly and whole-souled a party as you ever met. Jesus lived in the village with Antonio, but found time to spend many an evening with the boys. One of the visitors, I could see, was consumptive (a type of American refugee, alas! too frequently met in Mexico), tall, gaunt, with bloodless lips and cavernous eyes. "Tom is picking up every day," said the Superintendent, slapping him cheerfully on the back.

Poor Tom! He knew and all knew how near the end, yet he was as jovial as the best.

Three of the young men were college bred. They had all the old college songs and some new ones, and it was their nightly pastime to gather

on that portico and sing while the villagers below
listened, and the sombre mountains all around took
up the echoing chords, flinging them back and
forth until this little world of theirs was filled with
music.

After my long lonesome ride what a delight it
was!　The magic of their songs brought back
my youth and made that wild spot in the Sierras
full of moving memories.　Now it was " Home
Again " with its lingering pathos, now the rollick-
ing " Ram of Darbytown," Tom taking his turn
at a final verse which told how —

> " The hoofs upon this ram, sir,
>   They made them into glue,
>   Which stuck the parts together again
>   Just as good as new."

Chorus : —

> " Just as good as new, sir,
>   Just as good as new.
>   It stuck the parts together again,
>   Just as good as new."

Jesus did not join this, but his turn came when
the grand baritone of the young Superintendent,
the same that first caught my ears down in the
cañon, soared forth in " The Sweet By and By."

Oh, the ineffable, never failing promise of the
words!　The exaltation of the music!

The chorus of the second verse was swelling sublime : —

> " In the sweet by and by
> We shall meet on that beautiful shore,
> In the sweet — "

There was a sudden, almost simultaneous, pause,
and all except Jesus began a rhythmic, muffled patting with hands and knees.

"Get there, Cæsar! Get there!" they shouted,
keeping up the shuffling time beat. What could
the madcaps mean?

"Get there, Cæsar! Get there!" Along the
path was approaching a figure carrying a lantern.
Soon I saw the unmistakable gait and features of
a negro. It was the huge, colored watchman on
his way to the mine.

"Get there, Cæsar! Get there!" Even Jesus
was now patting with the rest. The negro strove
to pass with solemn dignity. He seemed to resent
and rebuke their levity. But as if yielding to a
spell that defied resistance, he paused. Then rip-
pled over his face a grin such as God has given no
other race. Unconsciously his head and body began to sway, irresistibly his feet began to shuffle,
in spite of himself down went the lantern, off went
his hat, and he danced to their patting. And such
a grotesque dance it was! They cheered and

patted and patted and cheered, urging him on, faster and harder till he and they were exhausted with the mirth of it.

But the dancing fit was on.

"Get your banjo, Tom," said the Superintendent. Tom got his banjo and twankled away. The Superintendent himself (they called him Sam) first took the floor. He was terribly in earnest, face resolute and stern.

"Get there, Sam!" they cried, and he did, to their hearts' content.

"Now Doc!" It was the doctor's turn. "Get there, Doc!" And setting at defiance every decorous tradition of his profession, the doctor pranced, kicked, and capered till the grim Sierras shook their sides.

One followed the other. Would they spare Jesus? I became uneasy. It was unseemly enough in a doctor, but in a minister of the Gospel, — spare him? No! "Get there, Jesus!" And let it be recorded, Jesus got there.

No lineal ancestor of Don Patricio at a wake ever stepped it more sprightly. None of his Spanish kindred were ever more graceful at a fandango, and, oh that it must be told! there was a certain uncouth fury in some of his motions, accented now and then by a wild, ringing whoop that told too plainly of the aborigine.

CHAPTER XXXIII

A PROSPEROUS MISSION

THE mission labors of Jesus at Santa Rosa, I learned, had been marvellously successful. From the very first the simple miners were well disposed. His earnest words, his kindly ways, won at once their confidence. Instead of a slow struggle to catch an occasional straggler, as at Alameda, he found here a whole community ripe for conversion. There was no malign influence. Not a priest had visited the spot for months. Indeed, the only visible trace of Rome was a ruined church built no one knew when, and now used as a sheepfold.

The ground was fallow.

Whole families had already made open profession of faith. The few who could read had Bibles, and from nearly every house idolatrous pictures of saints had been exorcised. Jesus beamed with pride in telling me this.

"In good time," he said, "I am sure I shall make them throw away their statues of the Virgin."

His first convert was a miner named Mendez,

foreman of one of the levels, and to Mendez' influence and example Jesus attributed much of his success. It gave me great satisfaction to see him so enthusiastic.

I went to the first service held after my arrival. It was in the open air, and it seemed as if the whole population was in attendance. Doubtless many of them came through curiosity, but there was surely a large number like Mendez, thoroughly sincere. Jesus prayed and Mendez prayed. Then followed a song. The singing at first was timid and scattering, but took heart at the second verse, increasing and strengthening still more at the third, and swelling magnificently thereafter. They are fond of music, those Mexicans, and know a good song when they hear it. To me, however, it took away a great deal of the effect to hear "Hold the fort, for I am coming," given as "Mantened el baluarte que ya vengo," and it seemed like sacrilege to sing "The sweet by and by" to the words "Dulce mas alla." But I got used to it, although I stuck to the good old English text myself, even if I did confuse the black-faced chaps about me.

Jesus preached in Spanish. The lad is undoubtedly an orator in that language, fervent, graceful, fluent. They hung on his words. I saw women weep and the faces of men sadden. There were sobs at times, and when he knelt to pray, the multitude knelt with him. My soul kindled. I felt more satisfied then with missionary work than at any time since coming to Mexico.

"There will be a spiritual revolution in Santa Rosa," said I to the boys that night. "Can you not see a change already in the habits of those men?"

"I see a change in some of them," said Mowry, "they are inclined to shirk work on the pretext of going to prayer meeting."

Mowry, I perceived, while a good fellow in his way, was rather inclined to cynicism.

"Well," said I, "the change may not come as quickly as I think, but come it will. Those songs and prayers such as I heard to-night — "

"Go in one ear and out of the other," said Mowry. "You cannot with a song or a prayer change constitutional conditions. Those greasers will remain substantially as nature made them, whatever their temporary emotions.

"What good," he continued, "has singing and praying done for our own Indians?"

"What do you say if we try what good a song will do for ourselves?" said the Superintendent, and on the word his baritone once more rang out, "I was seeing Nelly home."

CHAPTER XXXIV

THE ACCIDENT

I LIKED my stay at Santa Rosa. Not to speak of the pleasant companionship of my hosts, nor the great interest I took in the mission, it was rare enjoyment to sit on that portico and watch the sun-baked village below, the miners going and coming, and the little ore-laden cars roaring down the iron rails which led from the mouth of the mine. Night and day those cars went by, confirming my sound-money doctrine that there is too much silver. But what pleased me most was the constant courtesy of the miners.

I had seen miners at the coal mines of Pennsylvania and at the iron mines of Michigan, and they always seemed to me an overworked, gloomy set, sullen and ill. But these cheery Mexicans saluted me graciously every time they passed. I could hear their songs as they went to work before daylight, and I loved to see and hear them come singing home at night. Nothing seemed to ruffle their smooth manners. I saw one salute the doctor by raising to his sombrero a hand just crushed out of shape by an accident, and while the wound was being dressed, even while cruel stitches were being drawn through the quivering flesh, he smoked a cigarette or joked with his comrades, nor did the latter seem to regard him with any sympathy.

"Would you not like to visit the mine?" said Jesus, late one afternoon. It was the very thing I was thinking of, and off we started. A footpath skirting the little railroad led to the mouth of the mine. Here a huge engine performed the double duty of pumping out the water and lowering and raising the cars from the several levels. We stood and watched the process. Out of the dark hole which gaped before us would come a loaded car drawn by a heavy cable, from which it was skilfully unhooked by a Mexican in waiting, who leaped aboard to manage the brake as it flew down the little railroad to the dump. Another would then push forward an empty car, attach the cable, and springing on it when it reached the hole, be swallowed in the darkness. Popping out and plunging in, one after another, night and day the work went unceasingly forward. Detaching the cable from the car that came up and attaching it to the car going down was done with dare-devil deftness. Never had I seen brakemen couple cars with more recklessness or skill. As we stood looking, Mowry shot out of the hole as nonchalantly as if stepping from a street car.

"How deep is that shaft?" I asked.

"Twelve hundred feet to the lowest level."

"And the angle?"

"Thirty-five degrees."

"We're not working the lowest level now; it is filled with water — fully one hundred feet of water at the bottom of that hole. But we are working the one-thousand-foot level, and she shows up rich. Look at that ore."

A car had come up bearing the Superintendent.

"Do you want to go down, gentlemen?" he asked.

"Yes," said Jesus, "let us go."

But my mind had changed. I had some curiosity to see that rich ore of the one-thousand-foot level, but not enough to risk such a ride.

"There's no danger," they urged.

"Probably not; but what if that cable should part?"

"That cable would stand the strain of fifty such cars," said the Superintendent, laughing.

"Well, your engine, the machinery?"

"Are in thoroughly good shape."

"Come on," said Jesus. "Let us go down."

He and the Superintendent got in the empty car, but I still hesitated. Just then a car came up bearing Señor Mendez.

"Lo necesitan a Usted abajo inmediatamente," said he to the Superintendent, who was wanted down at once.

"Que sucede? Algo de malo?" (What's the matter? Anything wrong?)

"No, Señor, pero creo que hemos topado rica vena." (No, sir, but I believe we have struck a rich vein.)

"Well, let us go," said the Superintendent, and Mendez having no thought of me pushed the car forward.

"Come on! Jump in!" shouted Jesus to me. Mendez turned.

The car was already on the verge.

I shook my head.

Mendez gave a final shove and the car plunged downward — without the cable.

I heard the awful shriek of the doomed men and lost consciousness, but only for an instant.

Coupling the cable to a car, Mowry and a miner sprang into it and I went with them.

Down that awful descent we went, the darkness relieved only by a feeble candle in the cap of the miner.

P

" There is no hope for them," Mowry whispered. "None! Dashed to death!" and the strong man whom we had called cynical sobbed aloud.

Down, ever down, passing the different levels, at each of which were horror-stricken faces whose staring eyes flashed upon us. Then the speed of our descent slackened, slower, more slowly, while the cable creaked and groaned.

"We are nearing the end. O God, what a fate!" said Mowry.

We could see below the cold gleaming water. We strained our eyes. "Sam!" shouted Mowry. "Sam!"

We listened.

No answer. No sound save the groan of the cable.

"Jesus!" I shouted. "Jesus!"

"Safe!!!"

It was his voice! Thank God!

And there he was with the head of the Superintendent on his lap and the body of Mendez lying motionless beside them.

How we got all three into the car, signalled, and rose to life and light again, I will never remember. One thought only filled my heart to bursting, Jesus was uninjured!

He could only tell us of the heavy car with its

human freight dashing down that sheer descent, but of the dreadful plunge into the water he had no memory whatever. He could not even recall how he or his companions reached the place where we found them.

The Superintendent soon recovered consciousness. He had escaped with a few bruises. But poor Mendez! His spine was fatally hurt.

"He may live a day," said the doctor; "there is no hope."

We stood about him while the doctor labored to restore consciousness. Jesus refused to leave, even at the doctor's order, but sat chafing the cold hands and gazing pitifully on the pale face. Soon the lids trembled, lifted, the eyes wandered vaguely for a while, then closed.

A spasm of agony. Again the eyes opened, and this time rested on Jesus. Never will I forget their shuddering terror. He drew away his hands convulsively.

"Un Padre!" he murmured. "Mandenme un Padre!"

He was calling for a priest.

Jesus bent forward with words of sympathy and spiritual consolation.

"Pon tu fe en Dios y no en los hombres," he

said, telling him to put his faith in God, not in man, but Mendez repulsed him.

"Estoy muriendo! Manden por un Padre!" (I am dying! Send for a priest!) Still that cry for the priest!

In the fear and agony of death the ancient faith had triumphed.

"Un Padre!" he shrieked. "Demonio, quieres mandar mi alma al infierno con todos sus pecados? Un Padre!" (Devil! Do you want to send my soul to hell with all its sins?)

Jesus rose. He was very pale.

"Si, Hermano, tendras un padre, yo te lo buscaré.

"He shall have a priest. I myself will go for one," he said. And without changing his dripping clothes he mounted a horse and flew down the trail.

The nearest priest was at Barotera.

CHAPTER XXXV

AT the hour of midnight a vehicle drove into Santa Rosa. The horses, covered with foam and dust, drew up before the jacal of Mendez.

The whole village was gathered there — men, women, and children. In the vehicle with Jesus were a young man of clerical appearance and a boy. The man was a priest. He bore in his hands a large silver crucifix.

The boy dismounted first, and when his feet touched the ground he rang a little bell. Instantly every head was uncovered, every knee bent, and the priest passed through the prostrate crowd on his way to the dying man.

"Let us go, Jesus," I said.

He looked up at me, then at the kneeling multitude — the same people he had addressed the night before and to whom he had been denouncing superstition. He sighed, passed his hands wearily over his eyes and walked away.

Mendez died before morning, and was buried

according to the rites of his church. In front of his jacal an altar had been hastily erected. From every hut came contributions of little trinkets to adorn it, — ribbons, lace, even rings from fingers and ears. Here mass was solemnly said, and among the most devout worshippers I observed the active participants in the prayer meeting. And all day the young priest remained in the jacal while penitent after penitent came to confession.

That night Jesus was to hold his usual services. He came, waited, prayed, but his only attendant was Antonio.

* * * * *

We were gathered on the portico discussing the events of the day, when he came toward us looking downcast and hopeless. Nobody commented on what he had done. Indeed, for some time not a word was said. At last Mowry spoke up : —

"What a curious custom that is among the Mexicans, to make a legal ceremony of an engagement."

"How do you mean?" I questioned.

"Why, a couple who wish to be regularly engaged go before a civil judge, make formal declaration of the fact, and that declaration is duly published for all whom it may concern."

"I guess that's one of Mowry's stories," said the doctor.

"No! Honor bright — I read it in the Spanish paper, *El Eco* of Alameda, which came by to-night's mail, and publishes the formal legal notice of an engagement."

"Don't believe it yet," said the doctor, tantalizingly.

"Well, I'll get the paper and read it for you."

We were all glad of something to divert us from the topic which weighed most upon our minds. He returned.

"Here it is. Listen!" and he read in Spanish a formal legal declaration of the engagement of Señor Benávides and Marie Romero.

I heard a groan; Jesus had fallen.

The doctor sprang to his aid. "Overexerted himself," said he, "that long ride in wet clothes."

We carried him tenderly into the house, but no sooner was he laid on the bed than he tried to get up.

"Don't rise," said the doctor, "stay here to-night."

"No! I must go home," he said feebly; "I must go at once."

Nor could we dissuade him. I took his arm, and we walked from the house. He was silent until we reached the bridge which spanned the gorge.   There he spoke.   "I must see her!   I will go to her now!"

"Well, we will talk of that in the morning, Jesus; get a good night's rest, my boy."

"I must go now," he said.

"What!   Leave your work here?"

"My work here!   Look!"

He pointed below.   Upon the altar erected before the house of Mendez, and lit with a hundred candles, stood the priest in his robes holding aloft a glittering chalice!   The bell tinkled, the great crowd knelt with bowed heads.

*   *   *   *   *

Within an hour, the stage carried away from Santa Rosa the same passengers it had brought the night before, with the addition of myself and Antonio.

CHAPTER XXXVI

THE PADRE AND MY PREJUDICES

I confess to a prejudice against priests It
gave me a very unpleasant feeling to know that
here I was sitting with my knees touching the
knees of one at every jar of the stage — a position I would have to maintain for four mortal
hours. Yet there was some comfort in the fact
that his presence would be a safeguard against
bandits, and I so remarked to Jesus.

The priest evidently overheard me, for he
smiled and shook his head.

"I fear," said he, "my holy office affords you
no security."

"Why, they would not molest you," I said,
surprised at his good English.

"Molest me? Less than a month ago they
broke into a church a few miles from Alameda,
stole the chalice from the altar, and killed the
aged pastor."

This was news to me. I had always a dim
sort of idea that such wretches preyed on the

general public, and then sought and received absolution from priests in consideration of a part of the spoils. So I ventured an unobtrusive feeler.

"But these bandits have all religious convictions, have they not?" I did not like to say, "they are all Catholics," but that's what I meant.

"So has every immortal soul," he replied solemnly; "and yet sin and crime continue the world over."

"There seems rather more of this particular sin and crime in Mexico than elsewhere," I responded.

"Possibly. Yet considering that we have an Indian population of eight millions, we are not doing so badly. You have an Indian population of less than two hundred thousand, and your whole standing army is busy keeping them in bounds."

"You don't claim that these outlaws are all Indians?" I asked.

"No, some few are of a mixed race, just as some few of the outlaws in your Indian Territory, where in the past six months there are said to have been over two hundred murders. Americans ought to consider the Indian element of our population and make allowance."

"The Spaniards did not have that consideration when they seized this country and made slaves of the aborigines."   I could see he was a Spaniard.

"I will not defend the Spanish conquerors. The lust of avarice and power have always led to cruelty and wrong.   Yet if comparison must be made, Indians have certainly fared better with Spaniards than with Anglo-Saxons," and he smiled pleasantly.

"How is that, sir?" I demanded.

"Well, the Indians in Mexico are still a people, the Indians of the United States are nearly extinct.   Your doctrine in their treatment seems to have been that of your famous Sheridan, 'A good Indian is a dead Indian.'"

Jesus had sat silent and moody while we talked, not appearing to be listening, but suddenly he broke forth, "Better dead than in the degraded spiritual state to which they have been reduced in Mexico."

It was blunt, but to the point, and I rejoiced at this needed reënforcement.

"Who shall presume to speak of the dead?" said the priest.   "The spiritual state of any man rests between his conscience and his God."

"Yes, between his conscience and his God,

but not between a priest and his God."   That was
a centre shot.

"Sir," said the priest with an unexpected dignity, "you mistake the functions of a priest."

"No!" retorted Jesus, hotly, "it is the priest
who mistakes his functions.   Why should that
dying man confess to you when the ear of God
was open to him?   Why should that multitude
kneel at the tinkle of your bell and prostrate
themselves at the sight of your chalice?   Why
should they not see that the Father of all is
everywhere, His voice in the winds, His glory in
all the heavens?"   Jesus was giving it to him
straight from the shoulder.   But the priest took
his punishment gamely.

"You are a Christian," he said in his soft musical voice.   "You believe in the omnipresence and
omnipotence of God, yet when you are ill you send
for a physician.   Why?   Because with all your
faith you know the physician has studied better
than yourself the physical being.   When spiritually ill, why should you not call a priest who you
know has studied better than yourself the spiritual
being?"

Now this was an ingenious way of putting it.   I
confess to its puzzling me.   But Jesus promptly
rejoined : —

"We know, however, that the physician's power to do good is limited to his knowledge, and when he pretends a knowledge that is not his, he is a quack and a charlatan." Good! Exactly my idea! There he had him — a quack and charlatan! It was just grand to see the boy thoroughly at home with these great truths.

"True," answered the Romanist; "but as there is no need of the physician assuming unwarranted knowledge, neither is there need of the priest assuming unwarranted power."

"But he does so," retorted Jesus. "Does he not arrogate to himself and usurp the divine power to forgive sins?" Good again! I rubbed my hands with delight and looked at the priest.

"Not at all," said he, firmly. "A power delegated is not usurped."

"What! Do you deny that you told the dying man last night that his sins were forgiven?"

Now, thought I, he must either acknowledge the corn or crawl.

"I told the dying man that if his repentance was sincere, his sins were forgiven him. Would you not have told him the same?" he questioned.

Jesus was silent.

"I told the dying man of God's infinite love and infinite mercy, how he had but to repent and He who gave His only beloved Son for the sinner would see that he was saved. I heard his sins as the physician would have heard his symptoms. I saw as God gives me to see their gravity. I pointed out the only reparation left for him, repentance, absolute, heartful. I believed that this repentance came, and that my efforts helped to bring it, and believing this, I smoothed the last sad agony of time with the glorious promise of eternity. Would you not have done the same?"

Jesus did not respond.

"If the tinkle of that tiny bell," he continued, "called the poor unlettered multitude to prayer, if the elevation of the sacred host roused in their simple minds the thought of Him who gave His life for them, would you condemn it?" There was honest feeling in the mellow voice.

I never thought to listen to one of his cloth, much less to listen with any glimmering consciousness of conviction, but what could be said?

"There are doctors," he continued, "who abuse their noble calling, there are priests unworthy of their sacred office. But Christian men should never on that account deem all bad or blamable."

There was a long pause.

Jesus then spoke in an altered, almost apologetic tone: "I mean no reflection on the good priest," he said; "but I do insist that the soul in need of peace must look to God alone."

"Yet," said the priest, softly, "you believe that God sent His only on Son earth in the form of man for man's redemption.   God knew human nature.   Those who closed their eyes and hearts to Him opened them to the man Christ."

"To Christ, yes," said Jesus; "but let no man dare take the place of Christ."

I was glad to see Jesus had rallied.

"Christ," answered the priest, "delegated the continuance of His mission to His apostles, and they to their successors in unbroken line to this day."

"I deny such divine succession in the priests of Rome," said Jesus.

"We will not discuss that," responded the priest, good-humoredly.   "Your history and mine, drawing as they do from different conflicting sources, would likely lead us to opposing camps.   But let us see, my friend, if we can find a common ground."

Jesus shook his head.   There could be no common ground between them.   The priest continued: "Whosoever professes to be a minister of God, and believes in his soul the righteousness of his divine mission while working on the lines laid down by

Christ Himself and followed by His apostles, must do good."

"I agree to that," said Jesus, cordially.

The priest smiled benignantly and went on: "Such a man, whatever his oddities of dogma, is anchored fast in the fundamental truths of faith, hope, and love. For my part, while a priest of the Catholic church and yielding to none in my devout loyalty to all her teachings, I can take the hand of such a man, whatever his creed, and call him brother."

"Shake," said I, impulsively, and there I was shaking the hand of a priest as if I had met a long-lost friend.

CHAPTER XXXVII

MISS ROMERO AND HER COACHMAN

OFTEN on the way to Alameda did I renew my efforts with Jesus, but to no avail. He never answered me, nor even seemed to hear. Once, however, when I urged that the formal engagement of Miss Romero with Benavides settled the matter, he broke out : —

" I must have it from her own lips that she weds him willingly. I must see her face to face."

Then he relapsed into gloomy silence. Again, without a word of mine, as if forced from him by the heat of heart and brain, he exclaimed aloud : —

" She must not marry him ! She shall not ! " And his voice had a strange sound, and on his face there came that ferocious curl of the lip and the savage gleam of eyes and teeth. It gave me a chill of apprehension. What might he not do? But it was useless to reason. For the first time in our acquaintance, he omitted his usual elaborate courtesies in leave-taking. He walked from me almost rudely with long, quick strides, Antonio following like a grotesque shadow.

I went to the Institute and informed the Reverend Lamb of the abrupt ending of the Santa Rosa mission. He lost his temper.

"The fool! The ass!" he almost shouted, walking about the room. "He should be horsewhipped!" Nobody looks well in anger, and the Reverend Lamb as he spoke was actually repulsive. "In love! The crazy, greasy lout! The Mexican hound!" Neither in features nor language could I recall the bland, benign, amiable missionary, much less the apostle of Him who prayed for those who crucified Him.

After a while, by a series of alternate snorts and gulps, he recovered his composure, hastened thereto doubtless by furtive glimpses of my palpable disgust. But the harsh lines of his face were still uneasy, as he said with a whining voice and manner: —

"It is a sad blow to our hopes if the seed so carefully nurtured and which grew to so promising a flower should now burst to fruit — the dead-sea fruit of ashes. A sad blow to the Institute."

"Whom have you in his place?" I asked. There was a gentle tap at the door, and in glided, with the soft tread of a cat, Brother Baez, alias Doctor Medina. He bowed to me, but I did not respond, addressed the Reverend Lamb in Spanish, bowed to me again, and softly and smoothly retired.

I did not think it well to tell the Reverend Lamb my fears of some rash act on the part of Jesus: they were too vague. But I urged that he see him that day if possible, or, better still, that Mrs. Lamb see him.

"I have no doubt he is at his mother's house. We will go there," he answered.

Leaving the Institute in the dusk of the evening, I observed a couple strolling in the little park. I recognized Brother Baez and Miss Anderson.

That night I walked toward the residence of Governor Romero. Why? The memory of that fierce look in the face of Jesus was haunting me. It had grown more vivid, more alarming, until I became certain his insane passion would take some form of violence or folly, and whichever he might resolve upon, I was sure would have its scene laid there. Twice I passed the house. No sign of him. Again I passed, and there he was at the carriage entrance talking with the coachman. I watched till he went away, and, following, saw him enter a cottage. The lady who opened the door for him was his mother.

The next morning I called at the cottage. He was not in. He left word he would be back at

one o'clock, said his mother in Spanish. While I
stood translating this and putting into good Spanish a request that she would inform him of my
call, and that I would come again at one o'clock,
Antonio came creeping out of a passageway near
by, on all fours, a stick in his mouth, and two of
the neighbors' children on his back, holding reins
and plying him vigorously with small whips.

I strolled over to the plaza and the great cathe
dral facing it, for I never wearied of the beauties
of the one nor the stately grandeur of the other.
The fountain played in the sun, the trees and
flowers had on their greatest glory, but at this
hour few were there to admire them. Sitting on
a bench opposite the church, I contemplated that
wonderful pile. It is the evolution of three centuries of architecture, the rude adobe of the early
missionary, the rougher rock-work of a later era,
the hewn stone and sculptured marble of recent
years.

A carriage drove up. I did not need to see the
face of the lady who alighted, for no one could
mistake the incomparable form of Señorita Romero. I was sitting there still when she came
out. The alert coachman sprang to open the door
and held it for her. She moved gracefully forward, but when near the carriage she seemed to

shrink back and I thought I heard a slight scream, but must have been mistaken, for she merely engaged the coachman in earnest conversation. It was, anyhow, a queer occurrence. I could not understand how the giving of an order, however complicated, should have required so much time. Several minutes actually passed before the coachman resumed his place on the box and drove away.

Promptly at one o'clock I called again at the cottage of Jesus. He was there, and a marvellous change had come over him. The look of fierce resolve was replaced by one of buoyant confidence, the black, threatening scowl had given way to the light of courage and hope. He grasped both my hands in welcome, as if his joy encompassed all mankind.

"I have seen her," he whispered; "there has been no date fixed for the marriage" (how his eyes gleamed!); "it is to occur when Benavides is governor" (here his face darkened a moment, then shone again), "but he never will be governor! Never!" Oh, the shifting, uncertain soul of the man! Hot as his tropical sky, beautiful at once and terrible! In an instant he was all smiles.

"I saw you on the plaza to-day," he said, breaking into a gay laugh.

"Saw me on the plaza? Where were you?" I asked.

His answer was a meaning look from those expressive eyes, and that same merry, irresistible laugh continued till I joined in, and so jogged my dull faculties into recognition of the coachman.

CHAPTER XXXVIII

THE popular political movement, which flared fiercely for a time, had little life in it on our return from Santa Rosa, — scarcely a sputter. One by one the clubs formed in the first flush of public feeling had disbanded and died; not slowly and in painful throes of principle as would similar organizations with us, but abruptly, even cheerfully. The Club Progresivo alone was alive. It had made no money at the fiestas. Some attributed this to the devious financiering of El Pajaro, others (among whom was El Pajaro himself) accounted for it by the demoniac luck of "un Americano llamado Craig," who had persistently patronized their booth and persistently won.

"Something like fifty Mexican dollars," Craig told me, but El Pajaro put the figure far up in the hundreds. With debts heavier than ever, patriotism at every hand ebbing and sinking, their President, who had been the mainstay and stimulus of the organization, off in Santa Rosa, the mystery was that El Club Progresivo did not expire like others.   Well for Jesus had it done so.   But some lingering spell of the spirit he himself had incul- cated held an undaunted few together.   Session after session these sat and smoked with doors locked against creditors and talked of their former glory.   They had no money, no music, and even if the occasion arose or the authorities permitted, were not numerous enough for a procession.   Their only sustenance in fact was the hope that Jesus would return and again assume their leadership. Unfortunately, this hope was realized.   I was seated in front of the hotel one night when Jesus came along and invited me to accompany him to a meeting.   Having nothing in particular to engage me, I accepted without inquiry.   After a long walk, which took us into an unfrequented street, we stopped at a two-story structure, from the upper windows of which a dim light blinked warily.   As- cending suspicious-looking stairs, we found our- selves in deep darkness in a narrow hallway.   I was uneasy, but Jesus knew his whereabouts and gave three sharp taps.   We heard a murmur of voices, then a slow step, and presently a slide in the door opened, disclosing the familiar physiog- nomy of El Pajaro.

"Quien es ? " he asked gruffly.

"Jesus," answered my companion.

"Jesus !" repeated El Pajaro, thrusting his face full into the aperture, "Jesus !" and withdrawing it excitedly we heard him shout the name to those within. There was noise of tumbling chairs and trampling feet and many voices — the door flew open, and in an instant we were on the inside surrounded by a dozen men, each struggling to get the earliest embrace of Jesus. El Pajaro first seized him and hugged and kissed and cried and kissed again, until another dragged him off and took his place. It was bewildering. But worst of all, El Pajaro, when torn from his victim, fell upon me and in a paroxysm of hilarious joy waltzed me around the room, then delivered me up to another who did the same, and then to the next, until, seeing that every one who welcomed Jesus with an embrace was bound to work off the remainder of his enthusiasm in a wild dance with me, I fled precipitately from this den of madmen.

Jesus came round next morning, apologetic yet jubilant.

"You must pardon something to the spirit of liberty," he said. "Are they not loving, loyal comrades ? I wish you knew them as I do."

I was not desirous of closer acquaintance, but said nothing.

"They have held together while weaker hearts lost faith and courage. They alone are left of the mighty army once enrolled; but with this faithful band I have the nucleus of a mightier army still. Patriotism has not died — it has slept — it has rested — it is ready now to rouse once more for motherland." There he was speechifying again, brimful of rank nonsense. Of course I reasoned with him. Indeed, I thought for a while as I argued he was becoming convinced. He admitted that in a political contest mere patriotism of that sort didn't count — it was without influence — without votes, and meant nothing unless properly organized and directed. He admitted that organization was impossible without money, and volunteered the further fact that it was impossible without music. He admitted it was impossible without parades, and even added as an essential I overlooked, "Fireworks!" He admitted that neither meetings, music, parades, nor fireworks could be had without money.

"And you have no money," I ended, clinching my argument. He admitted they had none.

"Then," said I, "what sense is there in stirring up those crazy fellows?" As luck would have it,

two of the craziest of the fellows happened along
at this moment — El Profesor and El Pajaro.
Again there was a scene of hugging and kissing,
only a little less demonstrative than the night
before, but violent enough to excite my fears of
more waltzing, and I stole away.

CHAPTER XXXIX

A BULL-FIGHT

As I saw nothing of Jesus for several days, and heard of no activity on the part of his club, I began to hope that my arguments had availed to turn him from his foolish purpose. There was no talk of politics anywhere; a more attractive matter now absorbed the public mind. Instead of contesting by word or deed the election of Benavides, or discussing the marriage that was arranged to follow it, the good people of Alameda had become engrossed in a coming bull-fight. My first knowledge of this came one day when a band passed the hotel, followed by men on horseback and in carriages dressed in peculiarly gaudy costumes. With this procession were boys who gave out handbills announcing in big letters a grand Amateur Bull-Fight for the following Sunday under the auspices of La Sociedad Benevolencia.

"Funcion Extraordinaria! Ojo! Ojo!" read

the bill — "Cuatro Toros! — Tres a Muerte! Y un Toro de Jinete!"

The last bull-fight in Alameda had been for a pious purpose, leading society ladies were its patronesses, the best-known gentlemen performers, and the church its beneficiary. Full sixteen months had passed since the event, yet people still spoke of its glories: how the crowd was too great for the "Plaza de Toros"; how the pressure for place, despite the presence of the military, almost provoked a riot; how the ladies outdid themselves in the splendor of their costumes. The feats of valor, the prodigies of skill! How two men were mutilated, six bulls killed, eight horses disembowelled, and two thousand dollars raised for another tower on the cathedral!

Nobody supposed that the affair of the Sociedad Benevolencia would reach any such rank; the society was unknown, the names of the performers unannounced. But time was ripe for a bull-fight, people were hungry for one, and indisposed to be particular. Circumstances, which ordinarily might have aroused unfriendly comment, only whetted the public appetite. The very obscurity of the organization took on something of a mystery which each one solved after his own pleasure. "The Church is back of it," winked one. "Benavides is behind it," nodded another. " Some power is pushing it," acknowledged all, "else why should it be permitted ? "

For be it known there is a law in Alameda prohibiting bull-fighting, a law stringent and radical. Yet notwithstanding that law, the Governor himself, it was said, had accepted an invitation to act as Judge, and his daughter, it was also rumored, would be the Queen.

Hearing all this talk — little of any other talk could be heard — I myself began to take an interest in the affair. It did not at first enter my mind that I would attend. I am a humane man. While I like manly sport of all kinds, I draw the line at cruelty to dumb beasts. No boxing match ever shocked me, nor foot-ball, bad as it is ; but I have had to get out of the grand stand at a race in my own town, rather than see impish jockeys plying whip and spur on poor horses already goaded to their utmost. And it has disgusted me to see respectable men sit and cheer such brutality. But there is a great deal of cant in this thing of sport, more I think in America than elsewhere. It would not be so much like cant if it were consistent. But think of it ! Texas licenses prostitution in Waco, and calls a special session of her legislature to stop a boxing match in Dallas. New

York forbids selling pools at a horse race, and permits gambling pools in Wall Street. We see the passing of the close-clipped pug, and the apotheosis of the unshorn punter. Well, there is no accounting for tastes. In regard to bull-fighting, however, there can be but one opinion: the sport is utterly bad and brutal; so say we all of us. Yet I was told by Craig that American residents and transients in every Mexican city are among its best patrons, and in proof of this it was shown to me that the Sociedad Benevolencia built great hopes on an excursion from the United States which was coming several hundred miles to see this fight.

"Americans all go," said Craig.

"I can tell you right here," said I, "of one American who will not go."

"Wait," said Craig.

Alas! Human nature is weak. On the Sunday afternoon of the fight, I sat watching the throng on its way to the Plaza de Toros — street cars loaded, walks impassable, every class represented from the mendicant to the military, all eager, expectant, excited.

And their excitement was infectious. I had resolved not to go, but curiosity kept gnawing at my resolution until the little left of it was held by

kinks of pride rather than bonds of conscience.
Presently along came a party of American excur-
sionists, who I knew had travelled a long journey
for the occasion. Was I to miss my first and probably only chance of such a sight? I slipped in behind the Americans and was soon jostling and
elbowing with other countrymen of mine at the
box office.

My ticket gained me a place whence I could
survey the very interesting scene. It brought
vividly to mind boyhood's exaggerated memory
of my first circus. Of course there was no tent,
but lacking the canvas covering, there was all
else, — the vast crowd, the ringed arena, the seats
ranging round and up, tier on tier. My eye
first distinguished the division of sol and sombra. On the benches beaten by the sun, called
the sol, sat the poorer classes, — the bleachers of
the bull ring; on the benches within the shade or
sombra were the wealthier; and in the most select
quarter of all, boxes festooned with silk and
flowers held the beauty and chivalry of Alameda.
But most conspicuous, indeed so prominent that at
the very first glance it held the eye, was a re-
splendent throne whereon there sat the honored
Queen of the Bull-Fight, Señorita Marie Romero.
You may think that the sight of her in such a

place would have lowered her greatly in my esteem. It certainly should have done so; but as a matter of fact, it didn't. She never looked so supremely beautiful. My first thought on seeing her was one of gratification that Jesus wasn't there, for if he were, her queenly appearance could not have failed to heighten his irrational love; whereas I could now use the fact of her presiding at such a barbarous festival as another and convincing proof that she was no fit mate for an evangelist. I soon observed an odd change in the demeanor of the crowd. Outside the inclosure, striving for seats, and inside while being seated, there was an easy, gentle courtesy pervading every class, but no sooner were people in their places and settled down to enjoy the occasion than there seemed to break forth a very storm of vociferous vulgarity. No one protested, none took offence — it was in fact part of the festivity. But I shall never forget how it shocked me when a gentleman sitting near, and who I knew held a high judicial position, yelled to some one clear across the arena so that all could hear, a remark unfit to be recorded, and the one thus accosted answered back in kind. Indeed, there was a constant volleying and cross-fire of the sort between sol and sombra. Two full companies of soldiers

R

were present, and not less than a hundred police-men, yet no effort was made to silence the mouthy mob; soldiers and officers appeared to enjoy the billingsgate battle, if they did not actually partici-pate.   It grew louder and louder, rising it seemed almost to riotousness and giving me some concern for my personal safety; but at the very worst, the Judge (who was no other than Governor Romero) nodded to a uniformed trumpeter, and the bugle rang out rich and clear the signal for the fight. There was a clash of cymbals, a roll of drums, and amid the wildest cheering in marched the amateur bull-fighters.   Conceive my feelings when as the spangled procession halted to salute the Queen, I recognized in the first rank, gay with embroid-ered jacket, velvet trunks, and silken hose, Jesus Delaney!

CHAPTER XL

Yes; Jesus a matador, and with him El Pajaro and El Profesor as banderilleros, and other members of the Club Progresivo Politico capas and picadores, all masquerading under the name of La Sociedad Benevolencia! I wanted to get away. It was dreadful to think of, let alone to see. But there was no escape. I would have to crawl over the heads of those below or the laps of those above to get out of the accursed place. I had to sit it through, and a sorry performance it was. Shall I relate it? Well, the relation may serve to keep others who visit Mexico from attending an amateur bull-fight.

Twice the procession headed by Jesus circled the arena. Then all who were afoot threw aside hats and cloaks and took their appointed places, while the mounted picadores, encouraged by constant vivas, poised their long pikes for the expected charge. The bugle sounded.

There was a crash of broken timbers, a roar

more of pain than fury, and in rushed the bull. But such a bull! Not that fighting beast of Andalusian breed, fiercer than any lion and far more strong, — only a little stunted steer with scraggy tail and horn-tips freshly sawed. No wonder the crowd which had been frantic with enthusiasm first groaned, then gibed and jeered.

"Otro toro! Otro toro! Traigan un cordero!" (Another bull! Another bull! Bring a lamb!) was shouted from all sides. Even the ladies laughed behind their fans and the "sol" grew riotous. Sticks, stones, empty bottles, were pelted at the performers. Such a mockery of a fight! A dozen armed men matched against one poor, puny, and dehorned steer! It looked as if the mob would leap into the arena and hustle bull and bull-fighters back into the pen. The mounted "picadores" strove to make some show of combat. They rode briskly around the bull and pricked with their pikes, but the scared animal only ran, putting more dependence on his hoofs than his horns. Some wag threw into the arena a little dog, which joined barking in the chase, and the climax of ridiculousness was reached when Don Pepe, a local buffoon, perched on the fence and bold with mescal, jumped on the bull's back and despite its plunges rode it into the pen.

This was too much even for Mexican dignity — Judge, patronesses, performers, all were overcome with laughter.

The bugle blew the signal for another bull. It came. But scarcely was it visible when the "sol" again proclaimed dissatisfaction. It was a starved-looking, brindle steer. As it passed, you could see blood oozing from the sawed horns. Instead of charging on the horses, it ran from them in fright, and proved itself an artful dodger of picadores and banderilleros.

"Otro toro! Otro toro!" again yelled the crowd, calling for another bull.

One drunken fellow stood on a chair and delivered a harangue on cowardice. The vilest epithets were flung at the performers.

"No nos roben! Devuelven el dinero!" they shouted, demanding back their money.

Amidst the din I observed Jesus confer with El Pajaro, and the latter left the ring, driving the brindle steer before him. In a moment he came back and waved his hand to the Judge. Again the trumpet blared.

The door of the pen flew open and in darted a jet-black bull.

Great was the cheer that went up, for at first sight the crowd knew he was a fighter and that his horns were unsawed. Without pause he rushed at the nearest picador. The latter, astonished at the fury of the assault, made no effort to repel it. Only the thick leather shield saved the horse from being disembowelled. One after another he hunted the performers to their holes in the "burladeros," or made them climb the fence, while those on horseback were sprinted round and round in a mad gallop, until, as if tiring of the chase, he stood in the centre of the arena and snorted his contempt. The mounted picadores discreetly made their escape.

Taurus had the ring to himself.

Another blast of the trumpet now proclaimed the second act, "Clavar las banderillas!"

For this feat El Profesor and El Pajaro had been selected. Theirs to wait the bull's attack and thrust their darts behind the horns.

Holding in either hand a dart some twenty inches long, decked with gayly colored ribbons, El Profesor strode forth. The panting bull stood forty feet away. Plainly, El Profesor was frightened. His face was pale and his thin legs trembled. Yet, conscious that his señorita's eyes were on him, he stood and feebly waved his darts in challenge. The bull, however, acted undecided, simply maintaining a sullen stare. El Profesor took courage. Again he waved his darts, and failing to provoke the foe, he shouted valiantly: "Adelante, Toro! Aqui te espero!" (Hurry, Bull! Here I await you!) That was too much. The bull's tail went up, his head down, and he dashed at the professor, who dropped his darts and fled.

There was a groan of derision. But El Profesor had enough. Only the most persistent coaxing and threats could bring him out again. Out at last he came, however, with unsteady step and uneasy eye, ready to run at the first move of the enemy. But instead of advancing, the bull for some reason slowly turned until his tail and not his horns threatened. The crowd shouted: "Ahora! Entrale! No tengas miedo!" It was El Profesor's opportunity. Screwing his courage to the sticking point, he tiptoed timidly forward and thrust his darts into the animal's rump. A roar, a flash of heels, and El Profesor lay prone. He was rescued and restored. Nor was he without honor. Even while the air was rank with epithets shouted at him from the sol, he was summoned before the Queen, who with her own hands wound about him a gorgeous sash of the Mexican national colors. With such recognition from royalty, no wonder he proudly disregarded the vulgar abuse of the masses.

It was now the turn of El Pajaro. He was the best known of the performers, and by all odds the most at his ease. For he bowed and smiled as he walked forward amid a chorus of hurrahs and cries of encouragement and ridicule, such as : —

"Luzcate, Pajaro!"

"Metelos derechitos!"

"No tiembles, viejo bribon!"

"Es poco pajaro para tanto toro!"

The bull ran bellowing about, making fantastic twists and bounds to free himself from the treacherous darts of El Profesor, but they stuck fast, their ribbons fluttering gayly at every leap. At last the beast espied El Pajaro, then charged. I trembled for the fellow's life. But El Pajaro, to the wonder of all, stepped aside unscathed. It was done with a grace and agility that were marvellous.

"Ese es torrero viejo," some one shouted.

And so it subsequently developed. In his early days he had earned a precarious living at the business.

Smiling and self-possessed, he again awaited an attack. Again the enraged beast with lowered head and flashing eyes came at him, and when seemingly upon him El Pajaro deftly thrust his darts behind the horns. The feat aroused genuine enthusiasm. Caballeros rose to their feet and cheered. Pelados whirled their colored blankets around their heads or threw their sombreros swirling toward the hero; cigars, fruit, even silver dollars were flung to him, and the band played a conquering march as he was escorted before the Queen. But neither the excitement nor enthusiasm caused El Pajaro to so far forget himself as to overlook or relinquish any single thing of value thrown to him in the arena.

Another trumpet signal!

The bull is to get the death stroke.

All eyes were on Jesus, the matador.

Oh! the degradation of it! Where were the prayers and precepts of the Institute? Where the pious culture and lofty inspirations of the college? Where the sublime ambition for the lifting up of his race?

Sword in hand, smiling, handsome, calm as one who in old Madrid had won a hundred triumphs, there he stood.

Shame, curiosity, dread — such were my mingled feelings.

The crowd in the sol knew him and gave welcoming cries: "Viva Don Jesus!" "Ahora si!" "Bravo matador!"

The crowd in the sombra knew him not, but the

graceful athletic figure brought out vividly by the close-fitting velvet trunks and gold-embroidered jacket, caught their admiration, and they cheered in sympathy. All was hushed in attentive silence, as standing before the Judge, he thus addressed him:

"En honra de nuestra Reina, la flor del bello sexo, y para la gloria de nuestra bandera y de nuestra patria, mataré ahora este toro." (In honor of our Queen, the flower of womankind, and for the glory of our flag and country, I will now kill this bull.) It was a touching speech and won enraptured plaudits. One old señora squatted near me was so overcome with emotion that she almost swallowed her lighted cigarette. Some sobbed aloud.

Love and country! What nobler inspirations could there be to nerve a man to kill a bull!

Jesus proudly walked to the centre of the arena.

Now you, who have not seen the Spanish national sport, may underrate his peril. But let me say, the fighting bull can make a misstep of the matador his serious injury or death. To despatch the beast confronting Jesus called for courage at once and skill. Goaded to fury by his wounds he seemed to have grown in strength and viciousness. He was pawing the ground, lashing his tail, snorting, bellowing.   For several seconds he continued thus, his fury ever heightening.   At last he saw the foe and savagely sprang at him.

Jesus leaped aside unharmed.

Now stood the lad in splendid stead the training of his boyish pranks in Deacon Oldney's pasture. To run, turn, twist, to confuse and flout the maddened beast was sport for him.   Wild dashes, quick dodges, every move a life in peril.   At last the bull drew back, and the matador poised for the death stroke.   Man, woman, and child rose with the nervous tension.

"Ahora! ahora!" they cried.

A savage leap, a swift thrust — it was finished.

To march amid the cheering multitude, to kneel before the Queen, smiles from her lips and words of praise, to be decked by her hand with all the honors, what more of glory had earth for Jesus?

CHAPTER XLI

IT was a great change and a soothing relief from the savage sights of the bull ring, to sit with Craig that Sunday evening on the plaza, listening to the sweet music and watching the romantic round of promenaders.

One could not help being impressed with the all-prevailing courtesy. Not a loud word nor a vulgar laugh nor an act of coarseness or rowdyism. Even the outer circle of dark-skinned and poorly clad pelados had an air of gentleness and dignity.

"It would be impossible in our country," said I to Craig, "to get so many people in a public place without some exhibit of the loafer and the rough."

"Yes," said Craig.

"Here," I continued, "are fully five thousand people promenading this square, of every class and condition, yet we do not see a rude act nor hear an improper word. It is an object lesson to us. Conceive any such thing in Chicago or New York or London."

"Can't," said Craig.

"I tell you, sir, the Anglo-Saxon has much to learn from the Latin."

"Manners," said Craig.

"Well, that hardly covers it. There seems to be more than mere manners in this quiet cheerfulness, this mutual respect, this gentle, kindly courtesy. Don't you think so?"

"Look!" he answered, pointing to a corner of the square.

I observed a commotion. Men were bustling about a wagon, a drum began to beat and a crowd gathered. The drum grew louder and was helped by hooting and yelling. In a moment the plaza promenade was deserted, ladies escorted and unescorted disappeared, while the men all pressed for position around the wagon, from which a speaker addressed them. He was listened to with close attention and some applause. Then another spoke, evoking more enthusiasm. A third arose, and even from the distance where I sat I could distinguish the voice of Jesus Delaney.

I have said he was a power in the pulpit. But I did not think it possible he could be at the same time a popular orator. Yet such he proved. His

words made waves of glorious sound. They filled
and thrilled the very souls of his listeners. He
played on their feelings as on an instrument. Now
it was the story of his country, now the pathos
of her wrongs, now the assertion of her rights.
Tears and cheers were his alternate tribute. I
understood little of what he said, but there was
no mistaking his impassioned peroration, which
poured out the full chalice of indignant hate on
Benavides.

I never saw such excitement as ensued. Rage
found no vent in words — men howled, danced in
delirium, writhed as in agony, knives were flour-
ished, pistols drawn and discharged.

We hurried from the plaza.

"Well, I declare," said I to Craig, "I do not
know what to think of them."

"Reds," he growled.

CHAPTER XLII

SCENE AT A DEATH-BED

Since the return from Santa Rosa, Mrs. Lamb and myself had been trying to effect a reconciliation between Jesus and the Reverend Lamb. But Jesus kept out of Mrs. Lamb's way, and my own efforts were fruitless. We were earnestly aided by Mrs. Delaney. The poor woman sympathized, of course, with the infatuation of her son, but she saw clearly that his true interests lay in the work for which he had been trained, and with the pious man who had been his benefactor. She pleaded with him and urged him to go back to the Institute. She even sought to palliate his religious shortcomings by being unusually devout herself, punctual at every prayer-meeting, and active in every evangelical work. The Reverend Lamb often said that the exemplary piety of the mother was some consolation for the ungrateful conduct of the son.

I had had hopes that in time she would prevail; that the mad passion of the young man would effervesce, and all would be well.

The bull-fight made hope impossible.　The gates of his holy calling were shut forever.

A minister in the bull ring!

I did not want to see the Reverend Lamb.　I knew his rage would be terrific.　But a note came from him early on the day following the affair: —

I dread to convey to you [he wrote] the horrible truth, but sooner or later you must learn of it.　Delaney! Delaney! — he whom I sought to lift nigh unto the very Throne of Grace, to be the glory, the pride, and paragon of our mission, Delaney yesterday flew to the lowest depths of degradation by actually appearing at a bull-fight, not merely as a spectator (which were infamy enough), but as a participant; in fact, I am informed, the chief actor in the foul drama — the matador!

Ah! sharper than the serpent's tooth; but I cannot continue.

LAMB.

The part of this epistle which struck me most closely was its reference to mere appearing at a bull-fight being infamy enough.　My indisposition to meet the Reverend Lamb became materially aggravated.

How true it is that misfortunes are birds of a feather.

Even while holding in my hand the note of Reverend Lamb, Antonio came with a note from Jesus, telling me his mother was dying.　Dying! I had not heard of her being ill.

"Muy malo para Jesus," said Antonio.

Poor Jesus! The message chased away all my resentment, and left naught but pity. I knew his love for his mother, and how her loss would leave him utterly alone. It occurred to me, however, that this calamity might be the God-appointed means for curing him of his craze and reconciling him to the Reverend Lamb.

I started for the Institue.

They had not heard of the illness of Mrs. Delaney, and were deeply affected. Even the Reverend Lamb was shocked into momentary sympathy for the son. Mrs. Lamb hurried to finish certain necessary work with which she was engaged, and urged her husband to lose no time.

"Go to her at once," said she. "She doubtless will wish us by her at the last sad agony. I will follow presently."

I went with him and soon we reached the little cottage. The door was ajar. We entered. Jesus sat by himself, his head bowed down. The door of an adjoining room was open and we could look within. On the low bed the mother lay, holding in her hands a cross; beside her knelt — a priest, Padre Pablo!

The Reverend Lamb paled. His lips twitched —his hands opened and closed convulsively.

s

Walking up to Jesus, he grasped him by the collar as one would a cowering hound.

"You!" he hissed. "You allow this!"

Jesus raised his eyes; there was more in them of weariness and wonder than of resentment. The Reverend Lamb's rage flared in its fierceness.

"Look!" he said, pointing into the room, "that vile woman —"

My God! What could have made the man use such a phrase at such a time! I myself could have felled him for it!

I cannot blame Jesus.

But the indignity, the shame which followed, will rest with the Reverend Lamb forever. I did not pity him when he rose to his feet and slunk away.

Jesus stood with face aflame, his fingers twitching, his whole aspect that of indignant rage.

He was still standing thus when Mrs. Lamb came softly in. Her quick glance caught at once the unexpected scene in the death chamber. I saw her sweet face cloud, but in an instant clear. Walking to Jesus, who had not noticed her entrance, she took his hand. His eyes met hers, and as she kissed his forehead, his head bowed down upon her bosom and he sobbed.

The solemn service for the dying still went on,

—the priest's low voice appealing mercy, the broken breath, the moan of agony.

I felt the awe, the terror of it all, and heard, as if answering my soul's own pleadings, the whispered counsel of Mrs. Lamb to Jesus, "Let us pray."

We knelt.

CHAPTER XLIII

THE MANDATE

THE hasty meeting in the plaza against the candidacy of Benavides was followed fast by others. The fire of discontent which had smouldered, blazed again. Even the press felt the prevailing heat. Articles were written, letters published, fierce denunciatory placards hung in public places. Music, parades, fireworks, showed that from some mysterious source the opposition had secured money. And when the truth came out, bitterly did Governor Romero deplore the presence of himself and daughter at the bull-fight.

But besides money, which is indeed the meat and drink of a campaign, emotion being the air, there had been found a leader; not a noted statesman, nor one who wielded power by his family prestige, but one able, heroic, indomitable — Jesus Delaney. The name was in every mouth. He wrote, spoke, ruled.

Alameda ablaze, neighboring towns tinder, on all sides soon flared the fires of a great political uprising. But it was only among the masses; not a single man of prominence participated.

"Won't last," said Craig to me.

"One word from the City of Mexico and it will stop," said Consul Leech, whose grin, however, had something of uneasiness, while he admitted numerous despatches to the Department regarding the situation. Still he and Craig were right. The day of revolution in Mexico is sped.

When the whole populace seemed at white heat against Benavides, when demonstrations everywhere were most violent and threatening, from a central power absolute as that of any government on earth, went forth the mandate, — Benavides must be sustained.

Politicians knew that mandate and acquiesced. Merchants heard and submitted. Professional men listened and obeyed. For whosoever dared to set himself against it knew the consequences. The civil authorities became alert. The military bristled into menacing readiness. Then followed a formal proclamation, reciting that for the maintenance of law and order public meetings were prohibited.

I sought Jesus and found him at his house. Never had he looked so well to me. He moved and talked as if filled with the inspiration of a holy cause.   I showed him the proclamation declaring further meetings unlawful.

"What will you do now?" I asked.

• "I will hold a meeting on the plaza to-night," he answered, and his eyes flashed defiance.

"But you must respect the law."

"The law must respect the people."

It was useless to argue; he was a fanatic.

I knew what was bound to happen if he persisted; a meeting in the face of the proclamation would be rank rebellion.

I went to the Reverend Lamb and told him the facts.   He realized their gravity.

"But it is not an affair of ours," he said. "Jesus by his conduct has severed forever his relations with me and mine." Mrs. Lamb, however, was deeply moved. "I myself will go to him," she said, "and try to dissuade him from such madness."

"I will accompany you," said Miss Anderson, who still had some lingering notion of influence.

Mrs. Lamb never related to me the details of the interview, nor did Miss Anderson. But the latter manifested for the first time an un-Christian spirit of resentment.

"What could you expect," she said, "from one of his mongrel antecedents and "—looking viciously at me—"associations?"

The meeting had been called for the plaza, but long before the hour set, the whole police force of Alameda was gathered to disperse it; moreover, the word had gone forth that if the affair became serious the signal of a rocket would bring the military, who were under arms and formed in front of their quarters.

Craig and myself did not venture out that night, although I had hopes that the mere display of force would suffice. It did. Crowds passed the hotel, but returned. No rocket ascended. There was no noise, no riot, the meeting was abandoned.

My gratification at this was mingled with some surprise. Had Jesus changed his mind? Was he intimidated? The latter seemed most reasonable and yet was not in keeping with his character. Craig and myself were discussing the affair at the hotel.

"That fellow wants to speak to you," said Craig.

I looked up, and there, bare-footed, bare-headed, and evidently under great excitement, was Antonio.

"Jesus esta arrestado," he said, and without another word turned and trotted off.

Jesus was arrested! That accounted for the abandonment of the meeting. Arrested! It was a bold stroke of the authorities.

CHAPTER XLIV

ANTONIO TO THE RESCUE

THROUGH the streets trotted Antonio, and when he met any one whom he had ever seen in company with Jesus, or at his meetings, or whom he knew to be his friend, he told of the arrest, "Jesus esta arrestado," and trotted on. At the market-place, on the plaza, at the church, he made his sudden appearance, announced the news, and vanished. Jesus had bade him tell his friends, and such was the fellow's method. He vouchsafed no explanation, gave no details. Now he would pass a solitary stroller, stop an instant, murmur, "Jesus esta arrestado," and be off; now he would reach a group discussing the day's events, "Jesus esta arrestado"; now his bushy head and distorted face would be thrust in at a window, "Jesus esta arrestado," and so he went. But the news, by that wireless telegraphy which is ever in operation among the lower classes, had in many cases preceded him. Men tried to stop him for further facts, but he eluded them; his mind was loaded with that one definite duty, and he was discharging it.

The groups became less frequent, but larger. He reached a corner where but a few nights previously a meeting had been held. Here the crowd was so great, further progress was impossible. " Jesus esta arrestado!" he shouted hoarsely. "Jesus esta arrestado!" He was seized by excited hands, hustled forward and raised to a rude platform. He knew only his mission and announced it, " Jesus esta arrestado!" There was a howl of fury. " Jesus esta arrestado!" he again declared, and there was a louder, fiercer outburst.

"Que debemos hacer?" cried a hundred voices. What ought we to do? was their question to Antonio.

Antonio scarcely understood. He tried to get down, but the crowd was too close.

"Que debemos hacer?" they shouted again.

The one wish of Antonio's heart sprung to his lips: —

"Vamos a la carcel!" (Let us go to the jail!) " Vamos a la carcel," he called.

Instantly an opening was made for him. He passed through amid cheers, the crowd closed — he was its leader.

"Vamos a la carcel!" all took up the cry.
"Vamos a la carcel!" Stragglers fell in, cantinas
emptied out. The mob, for it had become a mob,
swelled to startling bulk, now choking the narrow
street, now rolling rapidly onward. A couple of
mounted officers, hearing the clamor, came dashing up and were engulfed. A whole police squad
was next overpowered. Soon the jail was reached.
It was unprepared for an attack. The Fat Official
dozing at his desk, the few policemen on watch,
were hardly roused by the noise before they were
seized, beaten senseless, and the mob had full
possession. Doors were crushed open and prisoners released indiscriminately, until at last they
found Jesus. Whether he knew the folly of what
had been done I cannot say, but it was too late
to stop it. A mob's love is almost as dangerous
as its hate. All tried to embrace him at once, so
that only his great strength saved him from suffo-
cation. He was lifted bodily and borne in triumph
out into the street and the main plaza.

Here he addressed the multitude. With such
an audience, under such circumstances, who could
maintain discretion? Certainly not one of the hot
blood of Jesus. Before him the people, the sole
source of power, the sovereigns, the creators of
law. They had liberated him from the clutch of

tyranny. They had defeated the machinations of priestcraft; they had shown themselves the masters and not the slaves of men like Benavides. The hated name evoked a fearful demonstration.

It was sublime.

No wonder Jesus felt a sense of power, an assurance of success such as he never felt before. No wonder his dreams of ambition took definite hope of greatness. Far as the eye could reach that human sea roared and surged. What could withstand its power, its passion?

What?

A hissing sound assailed the ear. It was a rocket which rose and burst into sparks against the sky. Every face was upturned — every voice hushed — the sea was instantly calm.

Then sharp and menacing came the stirring call of the bugle.

At the very first peal a commotion could be observed — there was a distinct movement backward — a general turning round.

"Los soldados!" was whispered. "Los soldados!" some murmured. "Los soldados vienen. Corren!" came a frightened outcry. It was the soldiers.

There was none of that sullen, Anglo-Saxon obstinacy which scoffs the menace of force and defies shot and steel. An instant panic seized the multitude; every man for himself. Ere the single company of uniformed men appeared at the other end of the plaza, Jesus was alone.

No; not altogether alone, for as he leaped from the abandoned platform, he descried Antonio squatted on the ground and fast asleep.

CHAPTER XLV

A TERRIFIED CONSUL

WHEN the mob was passing the hotel on its way to attack the jail, a few of the rougher pelados ran into the office flourishing weapons. Some articles of value were carried off and a large plate-glass mirror was shattered. The guests were greatly frightened. None knew what would come next. Stories of plunder, robbery, arson, and murder ran from tongue to tongue. The jail had been sacked! The police overpowered! The military had joined the mob! It was no longer a riot but a revolution! Craig, who was in his talkative mood, dwelt on the accelerative speed of such affairs and the great peril to life and property, particularly for foreigners. Having confidence in his knowledge of Mexico, as had the other American guests (three lady tourists), all became concerned for personal safety. We consulted together and concluded to send word to Leech and demand his protection as our consul. Craig volunteered to take the message to the consul's house, and soon returned with the news that Leech was at the consulate with his family.

"I never saw a man so scared in my life," he said. "Instead of his protecting us, he wants us to come and protect him. He has sent messages to the police and the military."

So the three ladies, escorted by Craig and myself, went to the consulate. We had difficulty getting in, for the door was locked, and I believe Leech was so frightened he could not find the key-hole. But finally we were admitted.

There was no sign of disorder near the consulate. We sat there while Craig told such harrowing tales of his personal experience in similar uprisings that again and again Leech rose with white face and pallid lips to ring up the military. But he got no response. After some time Craig and myself ventured out to reconnoitre. Not a soul was stirring; we could hear the wild cheers of the crowd on the plaza. These increased as we went on and finally became almost deafening. At that moment a rocket went up, illuminating the heavens. The cheering slackened, then ceased, and all was silent. We walked down the street for some distance, surprised at the quietude. Soon we met a man running and crying: "Los soldados! Ya viene la tropa! Los Mochos!" Another followed, a pair, a panting, wild-eyed rush of fugitives. The number grew so rapidly, so great, it was appalling. We had to turn into a side street. We heard scattering shots — a volley — a fusillade. Realizing our own peril, we stopped in a sort of archway. Bullets hissed and cried close to our ears, threw up the gravel, buried in the adobe walls beside us.

"Let us get out of here," said Craig, and starting on a run we came plump against Antonio and Jesus. Recognition was mutual. But there was no time for explanation. Ever that hiss and shriek of hungry lead.

"Come on," said Craig, and, all following, we soon darted into the American consulate. We locked the door. Leech was invisible, but his voice, weak and tremulous, came from an inner room.

"Who is there?" he whimpered.

"Me," said Craig. Just then there was loud knocking at the door, and a bullet shattered the window.

"Come out, Leech, and declare yourself. This is the American consulate," I cried, but the craven groaned in abject terror.

"Abren la puerta! Abren la puerta!" (Open the door!) cried voices outside. Craig, splendid little man that he is, stood facing the door and called back in excellent Spanish, "Este es el Consulado Americano y nadie debe tocarlo a su peligro!" (This is the American consulate and nobody must touch it at his peril!)

Then could be heard the exciting hum of voices.

"Quien esta hablando?" demanded some one authoritatively.

"El Consul Americano, Señor Leech," said Craig, dramatically personating the consul.

"Bueno! bueno! Muy bien!" We were left undisturbed.

After a while Leech ventured into the room. At first in his fright he failed to notice Jesus and Antonio. But soon he recognized them and insisted on their leaving.

"You are not Americans," he said excitedly. "You will get us all into trouble. You must leave at once."

Jesus started to go.

"They shall not move a step," said I, impulsively.

"Not a damn step," said Craig.

"I would like to know who is consul here?" said Leech.

"I was a moment ago," said Craig.

This flurried Leech.

"But, gentlemen," he protested, "the consular regulations provide —"

"For the exercise of common humanity," said Craig.

I have already told you that a stimulant gave the fellow a magnificent vocabulary, and now he was under the stimulus of intense excitement.

"These are Mexicans," said Leech, "subject to the law of the land."

"And we and they are Christians subject to the law of God," I put in. "I protest against turning them out under such circumstances."

"But I must," said Leech, almost whining. "I will get myself into trouble with my Department."

Jesus came forward, his calm, intrepid dignity in striking contrast to the weak poltroon.

"I thank you, gentlemen, for your great kindness to me, but this is Consul Leech's office. I will not impose myself on him or any man. Come, Antonio."

Before we could interfere, he unlocked the door and with Antonio disappeared in the darkness.

We heard shouts and shots and the rush of footsteps. But it would have been folly to venture out. We could only sit and listen and hope while the dread night wore on without knowing what became of them. I learned afterward, however, and may as well put it down here.

They were seen and pursued. Jesus, who could

T

run like a greyhound, might have easily escaped, but even to save himself he would not forsake Antonio — the latter's short legs, therefore, set the pace.   Down the street they ran, ever under fire, and nearer drew their pursuers.   Capture seemed certain, and capture meant instant death.   Seizing Antonio's hand, Jesus turned swiftly into a narrow cross-street.   He knew he had but a moment.   "Do you know any one hereabouts, Antonio?" he asked.   "Si!" panted Antonio, "es la calle Santa Maria, aqui es la casa de la Señora Garda."   It was Santa Maria Street, and near them was the house of Doña Garda.   At a bound Jesus reached the door, and without rapping they entered.   To his amazement there sat Mrs. Lamb with a child upon her knee, watching while its sick mother slept.   "Jesus!" she said rising, "what means this?"

"Pardon me," he answered, "we are pursued; but we must not disturb you."

He started to go out, although the tumult of the chase now filled the street.

"Stay," said Mrs. Lamb.   "Hide here," and against his will she thrust him and Antonio behind a great blanket that hung from the wall.   Its folds had scarcely fallen when the door was pushed violently open, and an officer sprang in with drawn sword heading an excited file of soldiers.

He stopped.

Mrs. Lamb, still holding the child, stood before him. Even in the dim light of a single flickering candle, her tall figure, noble features, and crown of snow-white hair gave her the bearing of a queen. The officer knew her, and more than one of his soldiers had reason to bless her work. He saluted.

"Pardon, madam," he said courteously in Spanish; "but I must ask you are there two men in this house?"

What she would have answered, none will ever know. As for me I have no doubt on that point. Mrs. Lamb was a woman who would not shrink from sacrificing her very soul for humanity's sake. Yes — I mean it — her immortal soul if need be!

But, thank God! She was saved from so cruel a test. Before she could answer, the baby, alarmed by the strange invasion, suddenly set up a wail that roused the sick mother.

She awoke just in time to hear the officer's question repeated, and knowing nothing of the presence of Jesus and Antonio, naturally resented the imputation the inquiry conveyed. Such a vehement denial, such a torrent of complaint, such a whirlwind of abuse and vituperation followed, that the officer bowed low to Mrs. Lamb and hastily retreated.

He and his men were far away on another trail and the mother and baby were again asleep, before Jesus and Antonio came from behind the blanket, and with Mrs. Lamb's blessing quietly sped from the premises.

CHAPTER XLVI

THE WOOD VENDOR

I EXPECTED that the next day would bring renewed disturbances. But there were none. Everything seemed in its usual routine. The turmoil and
terror of the night were gone. The market had
its customary crowd of quiet, orderly, cigarette-
smoking loungers and buyers and sellers; the ordi-
nary traffic went on in the streets, even the plaza
where the rioters held their meeting had its placid
procession of promenaders. Only the jail looked
harshly dealt with. It had an aspect of fire and
earthquake.

The Fat Official was no more — dead of fright,
apoplexy, violence, none could say. His encoffined
body lay in the jail visited by the curious. During
the afternoon I chanced to look in and observed a
woman kneeling by the dead, unconscious of the
passing throng. She raised a tear-stained face as
I went by, and on it was a look of piteous grief
and terror.

Poor Lupita! No longer a child.

Six had been killed. One, a crippled beggar, sitting near the cathedral and keeping up his continuous prayer for alms, was shot through the heart. Another, an old priest who during the panic had thrust his head from an open window and was counselling peace, received a bullet in the brain. A third, a poor woman, at her fruit stand. None of the dead had any connection with the riot.

But it was over. Even the funeral of the victims made no commotion. Neither did the frequent arrests.

That phase of fatalism in the Mexican character, that Indian stoicism, was strongly manifest. An American community after such an outbreak would have taken weeks to settle down. Here, what was done was done; the masses were indifferent.

But the hunt for those charged with active participation in the riot was pushed relentlessly. Some had been conspicuous and were recognized, some had been formally accused, but the most sought after of all was Jesus. He was the head and front of the offending. The whole evil was charged upon him. He had designed the attack on the jail, sent forth emissaries to stir up the mob, and given directions subsequently. He had murdered the Fat Official, shot the aged priest and the poor, defenceless woman. Of these crimes he was accused in the public press, and they were aggravated by the additional offence that he was a missionary, an apostate in league with the religious enemies of his country. I imagined from the tone of the articles that a dangerous public sentiment would be worked up against the Institute, but there was no indication of it. The attendance there was as good as ever, the few converts particularly zealous.

Police and military were in active rivalry to secure Jesus. They were stimulated by the offer of a high reward. Every train leaving the city was stopped and searched. Every house that might be supposed to harbor him was entered and examined. Even the Institute was invaded, and every nook and corner scrutinized. But no trace of him. I expected momentarily to hear of his arrest, and arrest I was told would be surely followed by summary trial and execution. My heart went out to the unfortunate lad; but I could be of no service. My only hope was that he might manage to elude pursuit and leave the country. As day succeeded day without his capture, my hopes strengthened. Surely if he were anywhere in Alameda or the vicinity, he would have been already seized. A local paper made the statement that he had been seen and spoken with at Eagle Pass on the American side of the Rio Grande. This seemed quite probable and was generally accepted. I confidently looked for a letter from Eagle Pass announcing his safety.

Ten days after the riot I was sitting in the office of the hotel, an interested observer of the dickering between the American clerk (a recent arrival from Texas) and a native over a load of wood which the latter wished to sell. From four dollars the price had fallen six and a half cents a quotation down to two dollars, at which it was taken. But the demeanor of the clerk, openly violent and offensive, and the suave, gentle manner of the native was a study. No wonder the Mexican hates the Gringo. The bargain was finally closed, the wood delivered, and money paid, but the native seemed puzzled to count it. Looking about him, he came over to me asking me to count it. I did so and told him it was right. On returning it, I found a piece of paper in my hand which read, —

Follow the bearer. — J.

The native walked out, mounted his wagon, and was lashing his burros for the journey homeward. Without stopping to reason as to consequences,

I followed. The clumsy wagon and dull beasts went leisurely along until they reached an unfrequented street in the suburbs. Here they stopped. I came up. The native accosted me, —

"Señor, quiere Vd. pasear en mi coche?"

I looked at him closely; there was a familiar smile on the face shaded by a heavy sombrero. But surely it could not be — the sombrero was lifted — there came a ringing laugh — yes, it was he! My amazement instantly turned to fear.

"This is madness; you will be recognized."

"No danger," he said, and resumed his sombrero. The metamorphosis was complete.

"We must not stand here talking," he said. "To-morrow you can come where I am. Drive along this road until you reach the bosque; I will see you. Adios!"

I stood looking after him, marvelling at the audacity of the man, when a voice startled me.

"Won't you let me carry you to the hotel?" I turned and saw Leech in his gig, grinning. There was a mean leer in his face, and the eyes seemed greener and smaller and greedier. I did not want his company, but could give no ready excuse, so I got in with him.

"This is an odd place for a pedestrian," he continued, almost closing his white-lashed eyes, "an odd kind of place," he repeated with malicious meaning.

" I'm an odd kind of fellow," said I.

" You certainly have had very odd experiences, and got out of them luckily too — very luckily indeed — very luckily."

I was about to say " No thanks to you," but checked myself.

" Isn't it strange they don't catch Jesus ? " he asked.

" Very," said I.

" There is a big reward offered for him."

" I hope the poor fellow gets away. Don't you ? "

" Hum! It wouldn't be right in my position to so express myself; but you know where my heart is."

" Damned if I do," said I to myself, but remained silent.

" Of course," Leech went on, " he has made much mischief, violated the law, and committed great crimes."

" No, sir ! " I interrupted indignantly, " he has committed no crime."

" Well, I am only saying what is charged against him."

" The charges are outrageous. Time will show

the poor fellow innocent of any intentional wrong."

I alighted at the hotel and bade Leech good-by. Something in his manner from the moment he accosted me on the road made me uneasy. I stood and watched him as he drove down the street.

He stopped before the military headquarters.

CHAPTER XLVII

THAT night Craig called my attention to a policeman standing near while we sat talking. I looked up and the fellow moved off. Next morning I passed the same officer on my way to breakfast, and when I rode to the Institute in a street car he sat opposite me. It did not occur to me then that I was being watched or followed, but I remarked the coincidence.

After dinner I hired a vehicle to ride to the appointed place. I had no apprehension of danger, and looked forward with pleasure to meet Jesus and advise with him.

The day was very warm, not a cloud visible. Dust lay thick on the road.

I had ridden a short distance when I observed in the east what seemed to be a rainbow. I stopped to study the phenomenon.

A rainbow in a cloudless sky!

It was all the more startling as no rain had fallen in months. The drought, in fact, had been

so prolonged crops had failed and cattle perished.
But a rainbow it was and the colors glowed and
mingled gloriously. At home, thought I, a rainbow follows a storm; here it may presage one.
At the instant there fell a few bright drops. It
was a sun shower of rarest beauty, and as it
played and pattered, flashing and sparkling, the
vivid bow brightened and mounted from horizon
to zenith, while in the west the tropic sun still
blazed and burned.

The drops fell faster, and a sudden wind blew
strong and cool. I strove to find a place of
shelter, and turning, beheld an ominous darkness
bearing down upon me.

I was struck at once by torrent and tornado.
The carriage swayed, threatening to overturn, the
horse trembled in dumb terror of some dread
disaster. The chill of death was in the air. I
could but sit and watch the fury of the elements.
Great bodies of water writhed and fell around.
The heavens were an ocean in a storm — the
earth that ocean's bed.

I cannot tell how long the tempest raged. But
sudden as it came, it ceased. Cold and wet, I
looked about. Every trace of road was gone —
the level field which a moment before lay parched
and barren had become a lake.

I could scarce credit my senses. And to make it all the more weird and uncanny, there appeared on the surface of the water, almost within reach, a large turtle. Whence did it come? There was not a swamp or pond or river within miles. Did it fall from the clouds? The reptile seemed to hear my question from the wise way it looked at me and wagged its head. Then it swam slowly forward, and my horse unbidden followed.

The water lessened visibly as we moved, and soon the turtle was on soil where not a drop of rain seemed to have fallen. Here it paused as in doubt. Suddenly a queer, quavering voice called:

"Con-chi-ta! Con-chi-ta!" and the creature started off at once in the direction of the sound.

Along the cactus-covered field it crawled, now slowly and with effort, again with awkward speed whenever came that peculiar cry, "Con-chi-ta!"

I could see no one, but a short distance ahead of us there arose above the mesquite bushes a low, round hill, and it was from this the voice seemed to come. Nearing the hill, my horse shied and reared violently. There at his head stood a hideous old Indian, naked save for a scant apron of goatskin. He took the turtle in his arms, talked to it, fondling and even kissing its warty head and making horrible grimaces.

"Conchita carisima! Conchita mala! Conchita perdida!" he quavered in the thin, weak voice of age.

For the moment I was so startled I failed to notice standing near a countryman who presently came forward and greeted me, disclosing, when he raised his sombrero, the familiar face of Jesus.

But it was a serious face, full of warning and alarm.

"Don't stay here," he said. "Drive on till you come to the road and wait for me. I will join you in a few minutes." He spoke nervously, glancing with evident uneasiness at the Indian, who was still petting his reptile.

"Who the devil is this?" I asked.

Jesus bent forward and whispered : —

"El Sabio — the wise man. He is going to tell me all. He knows the past. He knows the future."

"What nonsense!" I exclaimed. "Why, the old beast don't know enough to dress himself."

"Hush! he hears you!" Sure enough the Indian seemed to be listening, and on his face there was a vicious look, half leer, half scowl.

"Dejalo esperar," he said to Jesus, who bowed submissively, bade me wait, and together they walked to a hole in the side of the hill, into which they disappeared.   In a few moments Jesus came out and ran to meet me.   He was in a frenzy of joy.

"She will be mine!" he cried.   "Mine! Oh happiness!"

"You're insane, young man," said I, coldly. "Some rank hocus-pocus —"

"Entra Vd. a mi casa, Señor."   The old Indian addressed me.

"He asks you to enter his house.   Go, and be convinced.   I will meet you on the road," said Jesus, and off he ran.

Now I'm sure I meant to turn my horse and go after him.   I'm sure no man in his senses would think of going into that hole in the hill with such a host.   But before I pulled rein, the Indian's eyes were on mine and (I'm ashamed to admit it) I followed him into his cavelike dwelling.

It's not worth telling what he did, — how he got a long horn from the wall, squatted himself on the floor and blew a low, monotonous sound to which the turtle turned and turned, darting its head in and out excitedly, — but what I saw when he handed me the horn and with a strange, forceful gaze from his eyes bade me look into it, I hardly dare write.   I have thought over it, dreamt of it ; ay! awaken in the night with the same shriek I gave when — I saw myself on a familiar street fall prostrate, and the upturned face was the face of the dead.

I reached the road designated by Jesus before recovering self-control. Here I stopped. The sun was just setting. Some little distance in the bushes a native was approaching, axe on shoulder. I heard the sound of horses' hoofs, and looking back saw galloping down a body of mounted men. They arrived where I stood at the moment the native walked forward.

My heart sank. They were officers and the native was Jesus.

But they did not recognize him.

"Parase!" said the leader. Jesus stopped.

"Que anda haciendo?" they asked him sharply.

"Trozando leña."

"Donde vive?"

"Pos aca."

The face wore a dull, expressionless stare. Had I not seen him in the same garb an hour before, I would never have guessed who he was. Even the voice had the coarse fibre of the countryman.

The officers were completely deceived.

"Vaya!" they said, ordering him to go.

Jesus started on. But unfortunately at this moment a rabbit ran through the bushes, darted by us, and after it at the top of his speed came Antonio.　All knew him instantly.

"El conejo! El conejo! Agarrelo, Jesus! Agarrelo!" he shouted.　(The rabbit!　The rabbit! Catch it!)

The officers sprang from their horses and surrounded Jesus.

"Rindase!" cried the leader.

"Nunca!"

The axe whirled like lightning, barely missing the nearest man.　There was a flash, a report, and Jesus fell.

Up ran Antonio.　He had heard the shot and saw his beloved master lying motionless.　Bewildered, he knelt beside the body.

"Don Jesus," he cried.　"Niño mio!　Don Jesus!"

They had no fear of him.　They laughed at his grief.

Antonio looked up, his grotesque features working convulsively.　All laughed again, and the leader came forward and laid his hand on his shoulder.

As if stung by a serpent, Antonio leaped to his feet; then before any could interfere he grasped the axe lying by the side of Jesus and with one terrific blow buried it in the brain of the leader.

The others threw themselves upon him. But the dwarfed creature had the strength of insanity, and struggled, foaming at the mouth. The axe was wrenched away, and still he fought with fists and teeth until pounded into insensibility.

* * * * *

Who got the reward? I never learned, so I will make no accusal. Yet deep in my heart lies a dark suspicion. God forgive me if I do injustice, but to me certain hands are stained with blood-money. Craig believes so too, and makes no bones of it; nay, told it to his face and the fellow only grinned.

CHAPTER XLVIII

EXECUTION OF ANTONIO

THE trial of Jesus and Antonio was pushed
with a vigor unusual in Mexican courts. There
was a general outcry against them, a clamor from
press and pulpit, from men in authority, from the
so-called better classes everywhere, that their punishment should be swift and summary.

Before I was aware of the imminence of their
peril, the examination was concluded and testimony
of witnesses taken. I at once engaged the services of the best criminal lawyer in Alameda. He
informed me that all the facts were conclusive
against Antonio and.very strong against Jesus;
there was no hope for the former, but proceedings
might be prolonged in the case of the latter; the
longer the proceedings, the more chance for the
accused.

"Then," said I, "prolong the proceedings as
much as you can."

"Delay is expensive," he replied. And I so
found it.

But nothing could be done for Antonio. He was clearly guilty of murdering an officer of the law. Circumstances called for a victim. Antonio was sentenced to be shot.

I tried again and again to get an interview with Jesus. But on one pretext or another I was refused. Finally the lawyer succeeded the day following the conviction of Antonio. I found him more concerned about the fate of his servant than himself; he would talk of nothing else. Not once did he allude to Miss Romero; his mind was full of the impending execution.

"It is murder — murder!" he exclaimed. "They must not murder poor Antonio!" and he paced up and down the cell.

"As well sentence a child," he continued. "Can nothing be done for him?"

I shook my head.

"God will not permit it! God will not permit it!"

I promised to spare no efforts to have the sentence commuted.

"Tell Benavides," he said, "tell Benavides to take my life and spare Antonio. He can arrange it, I know he can." He was irrational in this, but I could not calm him, and more depressed than ever, I left his cell.

The execution was to take place at sunrise on the following Monday. There were yet six days. I paid Leech for drawing up a strong appeal to the Governor signed by the Reverend Lamb and the ladies of the Institute, setting forth the previous good character of the condemned and their knowledge of his irresponsibility. I paid Leech also to go with me and Reverend Lamb to Governor Romero on the occasion of its presentation. The Governor received us with the utmost courtesy. He listened sympathetically to the reading of the petition, and at its close, after a few questions, assured us that he was greatly impressed and would investigate further. His manner was so charming, so benign, I could not help feeling encouraged. We left with strong hopes of a reprieve. That same day (much against my will) I went with my lawyer and Leech to Benavides and implored his assistance. Benavides, to my great astonishment, was likewise kindly and sympathetic, and assured us he would set himself actively to work in the matter, and, so far as his efforts went, we could hope for the best.

I was naturally elated at all this and told Craig, but he did not share my confidence.

"Why, sir," said I, enthusiastically, "I never in all my life have met such approachable, courteous, sympathetic—"

" Fakes," said Craig, but I knew his disposition.

Twice, subsequently, I visited the Governor, and each time I felt more encouraged. Naturally, as the fatal day drew near without a definite promise, I became uneasy. Still, even the night before, I could not but believe that all was right. The reprieve would come at the last minute. These Mexican officials, I reasoned, like to be melodramatic. I did not sleep that night, however, and felt nervous and anxious when I joined Leech and Lamb before daylight. We had been invited to witness the execution of four bandits, who were sentenced to be shot at the same hour with Antonio.

We reached the jail as a file of soldiers were entering. Seeing Benavides in the office, I asked if anything had been done. He did not say yes, but his smile was unmistakably affirmative. The reprieve was doubtless granted.

It would not be announced until the last moment. "It is all right," I repeated to myself over and over.

Governor Romero now made his appearance, urbane, beaming, pleasant, as if going to a dinner party. Indeed, all the officials had that smiling, serene, even jovial aspect. No one could suspect they were gathered to see human life deliberately taken by act of law. It jarred my very soul.

I did not get a chance to speak to the Governor, but I bowed to him, and the cordial wave of his hand and the genial expression of his face made me doubly sure. "It is all right," I whispered to Leech, who only grinned.

We moved to the jail yard. There was already the pale gray of coming dawn. The soldiers, with an officer, were drawn up in the centre of the yard, and a few paces from them was a row of five stools.

The officials were still chatting gayly and joking.

The dawn gained color, the first sunbeam struck the prison wall, a trumpet sounded, and a dull drum beat. Then from a low archway came walking out the five condemned men. With them was a priest in his robes, holding aloft a crucifix. Neither hands nor feet were tied, nor did any of them seem to realize their fate. Three were smoking cigarettes. All had a natural color. Not a single one trembled or faltered as they took their appointed places on the stools.

Antonio was last. His face beamed with the same innocent, boyish smile. It was a new experience for him.

He looked at the crowd, at the soldiers, at his fellows, and I could hear his low, contagious laugh.

A child given a new toy could not have shown more genuine enjoyment.

The priest went from one to the other of the bandits, praying with each awhile and offering to bandage the eyes.   One, a well-dressed, dainty fellow, listened devoutly to the prayer, but instead of bandaging took the proffered handkerchief, spread it carefully on the ground and knelt upon it.   Antonio seemed to think the bandaging a joke, and submitted as if it was a part of the game.   But every now and then he raised the handkerchief and peered out mischievously to see what was going on.

The officer in command walked behind the condemned men, pointed out the first victim, then stepped aside, raised his sword, and in a clear voice gave his orders : —

"Preparen!"   All was ready.

"Apunten!"   Each gun was aimed.

"Fuego!"   Out flashed the death blast.

My heart leaped and my soul sickened, as the wretch whom the officer had marked, fell heavily forward.

Those left craned their necks to see which had been the first, then nodded and smiled at each other.

Antonio was startled.

He lifted his bandage and arose.

A stern order, and he resumed his seat.

His smile was gone.

The game was not fair.

A sergeant of the squad walked to the body of the fallen bandit, rolled it over with his foot, then placing the muzzle of his gun near the ear, discharged it. The brains of the dead spattered on the living. It was the "Golpe de gracia."

Again the deadly ceremony was repeated — a victim marked, shot, mutilated.

Again, and yet again! Four fell sacrifices — four disfigured corpses!

Antonio sat alone.

He had grown more and more bewildered. He seemed to be studying what it all meant. When the sergeant approached the fourth victim, he had looked at him wistfully, almost pleadingly, and when the awful discharge tore the face to shreds, he shook his head in protest.

"Esto no es bien," he said pathetically; "esto es malo."

I looked at the Governor. He was smiling.

I looked at Benavides. He, too, was smiling.

Surely the reprieve was at hand.

"Preparen!"

"Apunten!"

" Fuego ! "

I shouted in desperation, but my voice was lost in the discharge.

I could see as in a dread dream the sergeant walk to the writhing body of Antonio, place the muzzle of his gun close to the poor agonized face and —

I fainted.

CHAPTER XLIX

DAY followed day, lengthening to weeks, yet no acquittal, no decision, no apparent progress. Now he would be taken before the judge, sworn, questioned, taken back to his cell. Again he would be confronted with the same witnesses, questioned on the same facts, and again incarcerated. The wheel of justice turned and turned as if its purpose were to grind the very heart of Jesus. I felt there was no hope for him — he must die.

Benavides' smile had a sinister menace — so had the dignified urbanity of Romero. The whole proceedings seemed a mockery. Yet it was my duty to do what I could, even in the face of certainty, and I told the attorney to spare no effort.

Nor did he.

The testimony taken in that case, the legal questions raised, the reams of writing, would cure those of us who complain of the law's delays at home. Every evening the lawyer brought me a copy of the additional testimony and the new rulings.

And I paid for the copy.

And Leech translated it.

And I paid Leech.

And officers stamped it.

And I paid for the stamps.

And I paid the lawyer for all.

But I did not mind the cost; it was the aggravating hopelessness.

Poor Jesus! Ill and worn and spiritless, one could hardly recognize him in the gaunt-faced prisoner who daily passed the streets, escorted by a file of soldiers, on his way to court.

He believed himself responsible for Antonio's fate. Often would he tell me of his dreams. "He came to me last night, Antonio did. He did not speak, but he looked so sad, so reproachful." And his eyes would fill and his frame tremble.

"I wonder if my mother knows. But no, she is in heaven, where no bad tidings ever enter — she is in heaven — if — if there be a heaven."

I sought to change the morbid current of his fancies, but words of mine were powerless.

One day the Reverend Lamb came with me. Jesus scarce seemed to know him. "Brother," said the Reverend Lamb, "bring your burdens to Him Who hath said, 'Come unto Me, all ye that labour and are heavy laden.'"

Why is it that on some lips the Holy Scriptures seem the inspired word of God, on others the hollowest cant? Jesus was in no mood for the latter.

"God! There is no God!" he said bitterly. "A fairy tale for children — a ghost story!"

"Brother," rejoined the Reverend Lamb, "do not blaspheme. Let us pray," and he prayed long and fervently, but he prayed alone.

"Debe Vd. vigilar mucho a este hombre," said the Reverend Lamb to the guard, as we went out.

"He is insane, talking of fairies and ghosts," aside to me. "I have cautioned the guard to keep close watch of him. I fear he may take his own life."

Alas! the same thought was in my mind. The flame of passion had burned, and the keen edge of grief had severed his faith in God and man.

"Señor!" it was the guard. "Quiere hablar contigo," said he to me. "Es triste, Señor, muy triste."

Jesus had asked him to recall me. I reëntered the cell. He still sat on the low cot, his head bowed.

"Aqui esta su amigo," said the guard.

"No tengo amigos," he answered.

"Surely I am your friend, Jesus," said I. At the sound of my voice he sprang forward.

"You must see her," he almost groaned. There was a piteous agony in face and voice.

"Tell her — tell her — O God! What can you tell her —" He sank back upon his cot.

Profoundly moved, I laid my hand upon his head.

"I will tell her you love her," I said.

He did not speak, but the gratitude in those eyes upturned to mine I shall never forget.

"Come now, Jesus, take a good night's rest. You will feel all right in the morning."

"Rest!" Oh! the pathetic meaning he put in the word! "I want rest, but I can't get it. I want sleep, but night belongs to my foes," he said. "El Sabio lied to me!" he was fierce again. "El Sabio lied! The charlatan!"

He was referring to the old Indian with the turtle, and I was pleased to see that his opinions regarding that chap at last agreed with my own. The filthy old brute! To attempt frightening me with his conjuring tricks.

"Do you know that I await the night with dread? In the day and the light I can think. But the night unmans me. Read this — I wrote it yesterday evening," and he handed me a sheet of paper on which were these verses : —

Night shades are creeping,
Where fair skies are weeping
  Their humid farewell to the day's fading light,
Sorrowing, sighing near
Me as I'm lying here
  Waiting the weird ones that come with the night:

Spirits all gloom
That come from a tomb
  That frees them by night and confines them by day,
Ghosts of the years gone by,
Spectres of fear that I
  Conjured up never to banish away.

Ne'er bringing joy to me,
Grief unalloyed to me
  Ever those ill-omened visitors bear,
Always they sadden me,
Sometimes half madden me,
  Sadden with memories, craze with despair.

Shades still keep creeping,
Where fair skies are weeping
  Their humid farewell to the day's fading light,
Sorrowing, sighing near
Me as I'm lying here
  Waiting the weird ones that come with the night.

The deepening dusk of the hour, the wailing of
the winds about the cell, the crouching figure on the
cot, all gave meaning to verses that might otherwise be meaningless. Queer uneasiness came upon
me — I hastily renewed my promise to see Miss
Romero, and left him.

CHAPTER L

A METAMORPHOSIS

IT is said the older we grow the wiser we get. I doubt it. At twenty I would have known better than assume any such unseemly mission. The folly of it! Undertaking to tell the daughter of the Governor, the affianced bride of another, that a man on trial for murder was in love with her!

The more I thought, the worse it looked. But my word was pledged. How was I to fulfil it? My former feat, the delivery of the note, was easy compared with this. Now I must not only meet Miss Romero, but meet her in private and broach a matter that may be grossly offensive. The day was mild, yet Reverend Lamb and myself had only walked a square or two from the jail when I felt hot and oppressed, and big beads of sweat rolled down my cheeks. It was not a matter in which I could enlist Mrs. Lamb; it was not a matter I could broach to her, yet it was Mrs. Lamb who came to my rescue. Put it down in your philosophy that there is no possible evil that a womanly woman cannot remedy or relieve.

We reached the Institute. Mrs. Lamb noticed my abstraction, and the moment her husband left us together she asked me, in her kindly way, what was troubling me. The question was unexpected. I must have looked startled and guilty. But the frank sympathy of that face caught my confidence. I told her all.

"Leave it to me," she said.

Would you believe it? Within two hours I was called by her into the parlor, and there sat Señorita Romero.

I don't know how she did it. I was not aware of even an acquaintance between them. But there was Miss Romero, and as I entered she arose with extended hand.

"Mucho me alegro de ver a Vd., Señor," she said.

No need to tell me that — her eyes and her low liquid laugh said the same thing — she was glad to see me. Was it the moon through the curtained window? Surely mortal countenance never before shone with such life and light and sweetness. It dazzled me for a moment, then saddened. No single line of care, no shadow of a lover's fate, that perfect beauty never knew the lightest touch of pain. What good to tell my message? But my word was pledged and I began : —

"I went to the jail to-day — I mean — hoy fui a la carcel."

Did my feelings trick my sight? No; there was a dimming of the dawn upon those fair cheeks.

"He visto a Jesus," I continued.

At the name she started, her eyes appealing piteously to mine.

"Jesus!" she murmured, "Jesus mio! Como esta? Como aparece? Habla de mi?" — the sweet face paled, clouded, the slender figure trembled, and, seizing both my hands, she wept.

* * * * *

Early the next morning I sought his cell.

He was transformed. A flush replaced the pallor. His eyes were bright. He sprang forward and embraced me.

"It will be easy to die now," he said. "She thinks of me," and he held up a tiny missive.

I could have known its very perfume.

How it came to him, what it said, I know not; but the effect was marvellous. Despair vanished. The world was bright. God reigned. What a glorious fellow he was in such a humor!

He took his acquittal as a matter of course.

He began to shape his future.   He would again take up the agitation.   Benavides would never be governor.

His volatile spirits rose and soared.   His cot was a throne, his cell a palace, himself a king.   I did not have the heart to chill that happiness, but left him in the full enjoyment of it.

CHAPTER LI

EVEN now my eyes blur, my hand shakes, as I write.

I came from his cell that day with some share of his hopefulness in spite of myself. What might not come from love such as his, such as hers?

I walked toward the plaza, feeling better than I had felt for weeks. There was a gay throng of young people on the street, and I joined them, almost as gay. They passed the plaza, crossed to the cathedral whose chimes were ringing merrily, and entered.

I went with them.

The great edifice was filled. I supposed some festival was about to be celebrated, for the altars were gorgeously decorated, and countless lights flashed on the gold and jewels of the madonna. Surpliced acolytes walked back and forth, and priests in splendid vestments could be seen from time to time leaning forward from the opening of the sanctuary.

A saint to be commemorated, thought I, or the Virgin to be crowned.

A grand peal from the organ, swelling, mounting, inundating all with melody, and everybody rose, every head was turned, every neck craned. Looking with the rest, I saw a bevy of little girls, winged like sprites, come smiling up the aisle, scattering flowers.

Then, to my utter consternation, came Miss Romero on the arm of her father, followed by Mrs. Romero and Benavides.

It was the bridal procession, and I was there to witness the wedding ceremony.

*　　　*　　　*　　　*　　　*

On my way back to the hotel I met my lawyer and Leech.

"Bad news," said Leech, yet grinning.

"What?" I asked apprehensively.

"Jesus is condemned to be shot."

Still rang the great cathedral chimes, the wedding bells, and Alameda learned of them love's victory; but my own listening heart could only hear the tolling, tolling of a death-knell.

CHAPTER LII

MRS. LAMB'S RESOLVE

I COULD not tell the cruel truth to Jesus; I had
not the courage. Yet he must be told, and at
once.

Again my refuge was Mrs. Lamb. Before I
reached the Institute she had heard his fate, and
I could see she had been weeping.

"Have you told him?" she asked.

"No; I can't! I have come for you to tell
him." She trembled and turned aside, but in a
moment she was calm again.

"I will go to him," she said, and together we
went to the jail.

As we entered his cell he rose to greet us,
eager, expectant, confident. The delicate perfume still lingered — his knightly heart was buoyant with hope and faith. Mrs. Lamb kissed him
tenderly, and seating him beside her on the cot
began, —

"Do you remember, Jesus, what made me first
love you as a lad?"

He blushed and laughed.

"You were brave," she continued. "You let me draw the cactus thorn and never winced. Is my brave boy as brave a man?"

He felt some evil coming — he seemed to see now the pallor in her face, the dread in mine. His breath came quick and he stood up, but his face took on a fierce pride.

"Try me," he said, and he looked steadily in her eyes as she also rose.

"I will try you, Jesus, and I have faith you'll stand the test. You are condemned to die."

His proud eye quailed not, nor did his color change.

"I fear not death," he said almost haughtily.

"But Jesus, you would not, knowing your fate, weigh down with it the woman you love?"

He strove to hold a firm front, but in spite of pride and courage the color fled.

"Be man enough, Jesus, to face the truth and keep no foolish hope within your heart — Marie is married."

With a groan of anguish he sank upon the cot. And she again sat beside him and put her arms about his neck and talked to him as to a child, while her tears flowed with his.

I could bear it no longer, and left the cell.

As I emerged, a trumpet sounded and a file of soldiers marched by me out of the inclosure, while another file came marching in — the death watch. A chill seized my very heart at the horror of it. I stood there dazed.

" Borrachos, Señor ! " — It was the guard who spoke to me, touching my arm and pointing to another procession entering the yard, the bor-rachos, the day's draft of drunken offenders. Most of them were familiar with the place and staggered to their accustomed corners. Those who could not walk were carried in by officers and flung down promiscuously. Some seemed new to the experience and surveyed the surroundings with befuddled curiosity. Others appeared to enjoy it and smilingly saluted the guard and myself as they passed, a few going so far as to perform a fantastic dance at sight of us. We are wont to speak of the same class at home as unfortunates, but such would hardly be the name for them in Mexico. They were on the whole as contented a crowd as you ever saw gathered together. They sang, they joked, they cavorted; they cheered for their own country and for mine, and when exhausted laid themselves on the bare ground and slept.

One differently dressed from his fellows attracted my attention. He wore black clothes, torn and muddy, and a badly damaged high hat. Despite the bloated features and blackened, bloodshot eyes, I recognized Brother Bacz. He knew me, and stopped in front of me, swaying from side to side. He strove to assume an injured air, but in spite of himself he would lapse into a leer.

" Ro—hic—Rome per—per—hic—s'cution," he muttered, eying me. "Thish work scar—hic—scarlet woman. Beast—hic—seven horns." He shed tears and sobbed, but the demon of strong drink mastered the demon of hypocrisy, and his sobs slobbered into a maudlin laugh.

"Seven—hic—horns! Wish I had 'em—whoop! Sev—hic—seven horns—Viva Bab—hic—Babylon!" He was mouthing and mocking thus when Mrs. Lamb rejoined me. She, too, recognized him, but the quick flush of disgust that rose into her face was soon succeeded by a profound pity. Even Baez, drunk as he was seemed sensible of it and staggered hiccoughing away.

We did not speak until we reached the Institute.

" Jesus is reconciled," she said, "but we must save him."

" Save him — the law is inexorable — we cannot prevail against it."

"Not we! But there is one in Mexico who can — one whose will can thwart the law when law would thwart the right. He gave his country liberty; his country has given him power. I shall appeal to him."

"You mean — "

"Porfirio Diaz."

CHAPTER LIII

MARSHALLING FOR MERCY

Of all the workers I've ever known I give the
laurel to Mrs. Lamb. Energy! She is the one
woman in the world capable of what she accomplished. Will! Why, we were all her subjects,
we just did what we were told. She it was who
planned the whole campaign, marshalled all our
forces, made every move. Yet she was always
the same, — sweet, motherly, lovable. The Reverend Lamb went at every task she set him
without a whimper; Miss Anderson stopped her
quibbling and silently obeyed; Nos. 1, 2, and 3,
catching some spark of her resolute soul, were
actually and seriously useful; even Leech smoth-
ered his grin and greed, and for the first time in
his official life worked without pay. And Craig
— sturdy, manly, honest little Craig — he was like
a tug dashing here and there as directed, and tow-
ing in some big liner after whom she sent him.
The chief influences of Alameda, political, social,
commercial, ay! religious, even those influences

that a few weeks before were clamoring for his
blood, were now brought into line on behalf of
Jesus. I have written "religious"—and be it
recorded here that Mrs. Lamb did not scruple to
enlist the Cohorts of Rome in her mighty movement. She sought out Padre Pablo, and Padre
Pablo at her behest, and with a zeal that did him
credit, went from priest to priest with the petition
for clemency and got their signatures. Yea,
more, I myself was present when the good Padre
came to the Institute,—think of it, to the Institute, and handed that petition to Mrs. Lamb, telling her in tones triumphant that he had not only
the priests, but had, and he reverently pointed to
it, the sign manual of his grace, El Obispo—the
Bishop.

In the common thrill of humanity inspired by
one noble woman, religious rancor was forgotten.
The press—and oh! what a petty, pitiful, penny-
grabbing press it is, not daring as a rule to call
its soul its own; the bar, as pettifogging, un-
scrupulous, and soulless a bar as is to be found in
Christendom; the pulpit, native and foreign—all,
or nearly all by petition, by letters, by open dec-
larations, asked mercy. Now came back to Mrs.
Lamb the bread that for years she had cast upon
the waters. Many a poor wretch whom she had

aided when utterly friendless in the days gone by,
had reached vantage ground of more or less importance and rallied to her, — more, who never
needed aid themselves, knew of the good she
had wrought, and stood by her. Public opinion
crystallized in the light and heat of that Christian
soul.

And Mrs. Lamb got the petitions and the letters
and the editorials and the sermons, — every one of
them, — and she arranged them for ready reference
and bound them with her own hands. And when
all was ready she announced that she herself would
present them to Diaz, that she herself would plead
with the soldier President of the Republic for the
life of the lad she loved.

I begged and was granted permission to accompany her.

There was a crowd at the train to see us off, —
the faculty and Leech and Craig, and El Profesor and El Pajaro representing the defunct Sociedad Benevolencia. El Pajaro took occasion to
embrace me, uttering voluble wishes for our success; too many pressed upon us for further demonstration on his part, otherwise I have no doubt
that as on a former manifestation of his good will
he would have waltzed me up and down the
station.

Many of Mrs. Lamb's wards were there, and they had flowers for her, and the poor creatures cried at parting as if she were going off forever instead of for a few days.

We stood on the rear platform of our car, and when the train drew out the crowd cheered. Ladies waved their handkerchiefs and gentlemen their hats as long as we were in sight, and even when all else was blurred by the distance I could discern El Pajaro, who, mounted on the shoulders of El Profesor, was wildly flourishing his sombrero.

CHAPTER LIV

THE City of Mexico is the Paris of the Republic. It draws to itself all Mexicans who have money to spend, and offers them ways and means of spending it. It is the centre of power, opulence, and typhoid. Nowhere on earth can be seen such contrasts. Along the street passed an endless parade of ostentatious equipages, each rivalling the other in splendor, footmen in gorgeous livery, ladies ablaze with jewellery, while the walk was almost impassable with beggars shocking in their misery and filth; automobile carriages whizzed by primeval ox-carts; horses imported at marvellous cost and horses that should be deported at any sacrifice; here a palace, magnificent, superb, beside that palace a windowless hovel, whose occupants lived without bed, chair, or table; clouted savages and courtly clad dignitaries; a constant carnival of extravagance and pride, a dreadful background of shamelessness and want.

But Mrs. Lamb and myself spent no time in sight-seeing. We were at the American legation before its clerks put in an appearance. The American Minister received us kindly. He had for years represented a southern state in the United States Senate and was a typical, old-time southern gentleman. He readily promised to arrange an audience with President Diaz and talked very frankly regarding him and our prospects.

"A great man, madam, a great man is Diaz. You will get a hearing, madam, but don't be sanguine. God bless you, sir" (turning to me), "Diaz is iron — iron, sir. No use to attempt to reach his heart, sir, none, by Gad, sir! I have tried it, madam, I have tried it — Cold as chilled steel, sir, chilled steel, by Gad, sir — But a great man — a great man."

We went next to the American Consul-General. My experience with Leech had prejudiced me against consuls, but I found this one not a bit like him. He was genial, cordial, almost demonstrative in his kindness. He looked over our papers and agreed to go with us to the palace and supplement Mrs. Lamb's plea with his own.

"It's going out of my way to do so, but I'm heart and soul with the mission cause," he said

Y

"and a constant reader of your paper." (He referred to the *Clarion*, from whose editors I had letters.) "Don't let your paper abuse me for it — you understand, eh "— and he clapped me on the back and laughed an amazingly hearty laugh. That laugh, I heard afterward, was the foundation and mainstay of his political career. It had won his way from the bar (where laughs don't count) to the Congress of the United States, and to the office of governor. Of course it didn't keep him long in either place, for at times either place is no laughing matter; but when he got out of one soft job that became serious, he soon laughed his way to another. It was a loud laugh, but mellow and musical; it won at once your confidence and good will; it pleased you when he told a story himself, and pleased still more when you told a story of your own. Even the Mexicans, who seldom laugh, were charmed with it. It was for them a lexicon in which could be found the most agreeable meaning.

While chatting with Mrs. Lamb and myself, several of their prominent officials dropped in.

"Buenos dias, Señor," he would hail one with his laugh.

"Como esta Usted?" to another, and a laugh covered his retreat from that other's response.

"Muy allegro! Muy allegro!" he would shout laughing to a third, and one and all pronounced him "Un Americano muy simpatico." We were indeed grateful for his voluntary offer to go with us to the President and aid in the presentation of our case. But he, too, warned us against setting our hopes too high. From none with whom we consulted did we get any word of encouragement. It was arranged that we would be received by the President the following day.

That night, walking along the streets lit by electric lights, I paused before the executive palace. Its many windows glowed gloriously. Soldiers were on guard at the entrance and patrolled the grounds. While I stood there admiring, a carriage drove up and from it alighted Señor Benavides. The guard presented arms and he was ushered in. My heart fell, for I surmised his mission.

CHAPTER LV

PORFIRIO DIAZ

Porfirio Diaz! Statesman-Soldier, Autocrat-Patriot, Imperial-President! Absolute Monarch of fourteen millions of people! To him we were to submit the fate of Jesus.

We came to the palace an hour before the time appointed. We waited almost another hour while deputation after deputation preceded us. Office-seekers, tourists, suppliants — I watched the crowd and wondered at the endurance of the man who received and listened to them all. I was nervous; my mind dwelt on Benavides' visit, and I felt that our case was prejudged. Even the good fellowship of the Consul-General who waited with us failed to divert me. He talked and laughed and told stories without getting a word from me; but I doubt if he noticed my abstraction — he was always happy in the sound of his own voice.

At last we were called.

I had seen pictures of Diaz and had formed

my impression of him, but a different man was now before me — a well-built man of medium height, of a complexion and cast of countenance pronouncedly Indian. The short, straight, iron-gray hair, the close-clipped mustache, the small, firm mouth, the heavy jaws, the strong chin, and sharp, deep-set, black eyes told of indomitable will. Cold, hard, fixed, there was not a weak line in his whole make-up. He stood like a uniformed statue in bronze. Hope froze at sight of him.

The minister had already presented our bound volume of petitions, letters, and testimonials, so the Consul-General at once opened the case. He was as much at ease as if telling a fresh story at a cross-road tavern in his own state. He spoke well, yet seemed to me scarce serious enough; indeed, he missed no chance for a jocular allusion, nor failed to round that up with his usual laugh. But while the President listened respectfully, he never once looked our way, nor did even a smile acknowledge the consul's levity. Ever that hard, impenetrable front! The consul concluded and an interpreter put his remarks in Spanish; but I was satisfied the President gave no more heed to the translation than he did to the original. And my soul revolted! " Does this

man with his sphinx-like mien know there is a
God before Whom he must some day plead?
Does this impassive creature with all his power—"
But Mrs. Lamb now rose to speak. She was
pale as death, yet her grand eyes shone clear
and calm. She spoke in Spanish, but I knew her
meaning.

"An American woman has come before you, Mr.
President, to plead for the life of the grandson of
a Mexican soldier." At the first phrase that fell
from her lips, articulate music, he was moved.
His lids lifted, his keen eyes sought hers. "I
plead for the grandson of your companion-in-arms,
your patriot-brother in the days of Mexico's sorest
need, Colonel Villareal." At the mention of the
name I saw distinctly on the old hero's face a thrill
of recognition. He gazed at her intently, catching
every word, impressed by her presence and plainly
swayed by the magic of her eloquence. She told
the story of the life of Jesus—his early poverty,
his entrance to the Institute, his final collegiate
course. She dwelt upon his noble qualities. She
showed that even his weaknesses were not the out-
come of a bad nature or of vicious habits, but rather
resulted from the hot, impulsive blood of his soldier
ancestry. She dwelt upon his love of country and
of race, his veneration for his country's laws and

for his country's ruler.   And lastly came her plea
for mercy for the lad she loved.   I had to rise as
she spoke and so did the Consul-General.   Inspired ?   Mexico's iron ruler yielded to the spell;
the heart of the man was touched.   She finished.
Porfirio Diaz walked forward, lifted her hand to
his lips and said in Spanish, —

   " Jesus was made for a soldier, not a missionary."

CHAPTER LVI

ARMA VIRUMQUE

It was the *Diario Official* that proclaimed the news. Elation had calmed to hope, hope cooled to doubt, and doubt was followed by fear during the weary days of waiting, when came the official journal with the announcement that Jesus Delaney, condemned to be shot by the Federal Court of Alameda, had his sentence commuted to life service in the army. He was saved. Life service in the army! It was not what we had prayed for, nor what we at first expected from the words and manner of the President, but it was an infinite relief from the doom of death, and our feelings were joy and gratitude. We left that day for Alameda. The glad tidings preceded us, and there was as large a crowd as bade us God-speed to bid us welcome.

Mrs. Lamb got an ovation. Craig alone of all assembled showed no enthusiasm.

"Soldier? Dog's life. Better shot," he growled at me.

We drove to the jail. Jesus was not there — he had already been transferred to the cuartel (the military barracks), and we were told that the regiment to which he was assigned had received orders that morning to move at once against the Yaquis. Away we hurried to the cuartel. Troops were already forming in the street, and all about there was the stir and excitement of a prospective campaign. We sought the colonel in his quarters — a short man, so fat that the effort of talking seemed to make him black in the face. He courteously granted Mrs. Lamb's request and despatched an officer for Jesus. In a moment the officer returned, followed by a tall young soldier. We did not recognize him in uniform; the stiff, peaked cap, the belted jacket, the coarse guarraches, were a complete disguise. But it was Jesus. Mrs. Lamb, unmindful of the shock it gave the colonel, whose eyes stuck out to the popping point, threw her arms about the boy's neck and kissed him again and again while they murmured in Spanish their mutual love.

"All will be well in God's good time, Jesus," I said as we embraced.

"All is well now," he answered, and then we saw how his face was lit up with a new sense of life, ambition, and confidence. No shame, no humiliation, no disappointment there: he stood erect, his attitude almost exultant.

"I am a soldier's grandson," he said, "and have always longed for a soldier's life. I shall earn promotion by doing my duty and fighting bravely for my country's cause."

"And the cause of Christ, Jesus? Will you not continue to fight for that?" said Mrs. Lamb.

His expression changed, he seemed embarrassed, and hung his head.

"Ta-ra-tara! Ta-ra-tara!" a bugle sounded on the street. At the first peal he straightened to his full height, squared his broad shoulders, and with uplifted head drank in the music of it.

"Is it not glorious?" he said, the martial fire sparkling in his eyes.

"Ta-ra-tara! Ta-ra-tara!" Another peal, and then on a sharp order from the officer who stood near, Jesus turned and without a word marched to his place in the ranks.

"Ta-ra-tara! Ta-ra-tara!"

The column moved grandly away.

CARD FROM MR. BROWN

This manuscript was found by me among the papers of my late partner, and I make it public, as such was his intention. It is evidently an elaboration of a diary of his trip to Mexico, the facts jotted down from day to day being closely followed, and portions (the reference to myself, for instance, written en route) copied word for word.

Mutual friends of ours to whom I have shown the manuscript, say that it ends too abruptly, that more must have been written, but diligent search failed to reveal anything further.

My own opinion is that it goes far enough, and what befell this young Mexican might have been expected. His case reminds me of a fable : " Once there was a good dog who thought that wolves were dogs run wild, and —" but my partner tells the fable in the very beginning of his manuscript.